BEST
GAY ROMANCE
2015

D1617576

Edited by

FELICE PICANO

CLEiS
PRESS

Published in the United States by Cleis Press,
an imprint of Start Midnight, LLC,
609 Greenwich Street, Sixth Floor, New York, New York, 10014.

Printed in the United States.
Cover design: Scott Idleman/Blink
Cover photograph: Celesta Danger
Text design: Frank Wiedemann

First Edition.
10 9 8 7 6 5 4 3 2 1

Trade paper ISBN: 978-1-62778-092-6
E-book ISBN: 978-1-62778-107-7

CONTENTS

INTRODUCTION

When I was asked to take over the role of editor for this series, long edited by the more or less irreplaceable Richard Labonté, my first thought was "Oh no!" immediately followed by a second one: "Well, why not?"

After all, I have written over seventy shorter pieces of fiction myself, put out four volumes of short stories and several more of "true stories" and my own work in short fiction has appeared in over fifty anthologies. Every year, I read dozens of collections of stories and novellas for fun from many different areas: from hard science to science fiction, tomes of gay erotica to compendia of forgotten nineteenth-century German-Swiss writers and yellowing packets of nearly forgotten Ming dynasty authors—books that often fall apart in my hands just as I am finishing their contents.

Who better than a short-story adept, addict, connoisseur and still-active partisan in a glorious war and battle, to attempt what's been called "the perfect piece of reading for one half hour to one hour: with a sigh or exclamation or chill to the bone at the conclusion"? Especially if I did my job right?

Besides, I know so many talented authors myself: friends,

colleagues, cohorts if you will, people met at conferences and book fairs, at pride marches and book booths, in classes that I teach and lectures that I give or that I attend, at group readings and at award ceremonies and at the parties and bar parties and cocktail and restaurant parties before and after those. If I couldn't come up with a bunch of good stories who could?

I did make some stipulations, as the entire field of LGBTQ writing has expanded so widely from say 1982, when my first edited anthology, *A True Likeness: Lesbian and Gay Writing Today*, came out and I wanted that expansion reflected in this book. The amazing variety of our good and excellent writers was on my mind, so I made certain that besides a general call for submissions, I also sent the call out to writers I knew, about sixty of them, and was not surprised when they passed it on to writers they knew.

I made it clear that I didn't care who the author was or how s/he identified nationally, ethnically, sensibility wise, by gender, or even sexuality; however the story must be about a minimum of two men. It could be a true story or a made-up story, anything in between, or anything on the edge.

And the stories poured in. With this result: the current collection includes stories that range from the simple coming out tale to the punk, bitchy, wildly irrelevant and the super-sophisticated. In genre they go from the Chekhovian to the Woolfean to the postmodern and beyond. They veer from the gritty to the fantastic, from the sweet and delicious and dreamy to the sidewalk hard and downright uncomfortable to read, from tales of missed or botched connections to stories of vengeance and yes, even a coolly sexy cowboy yarn.

Are they all romances? I keep thinking about the words of the Countess in the classic film, *The Women*. No matter whether she is hitching up for the eighth time or getting divorced for the ninth, she always comments, "*L'amour! L'amour!*" So, of course these are romances, even when the erotic encounters and relationships end up fractured and awry in one way or another.

And when you are done reading them you will perhaps see other ways in which they reflect our wonderfully expanded and diverse gay life and queer authoring.

Felice Picano
San Francisco

TRANSITIONS OF GLASS

Simon Bleaken

For Richard Johnson

There are moments in life where you think *This is it, everything's going to change*: the dream holiday, the new job or house, even the new relationship. But it rarely does. Sure, these events are milestones in life, but most of the time you stay the same deep down and just find yourself in familiar ruts in whole new places, and all the hopes you pinned on them for that wonderful new future evaporate like shadows before the dawn. The truth is, real change only sticks if it comes from within and those are the hardest changes of all to achieve. But sometimes life lends a hand when you least expect it to. Though those times are like transitions made of glass—you can't see them approaching. They pass you by invisibly, yet leave you forever transformed in their wake.

For me, such a moment happened with my coming out, something I had never planned upon doing. I had lurked in the closet for years, terrified of revealing the truth about myself and hiding behind a mask of asexual pretence so thin I was stunned that nobody saw through it. The thought of coming out seemed less and less likely with each passing year, and I had grown oddly comfortable in hiding. So I quietly watched from the sidelines, contenting myself with private fantasies, certain in my belief that the world and the friends I held dear would reject me if they found out I was gay.

But nature can only be denied for so long, and the cracks soon began to appear. I was lonely, more so each year, and the sensual fantasies that I conjured in my mind when I returned home from a long day at the office never satisfied for long before I began to crave the actual touch and company of another man. And that, it turned out, was finally my undoing—in the best way possible.

We had shuffled out of the conference room like swarm of demoralized drones after the end of another dreary Monday-morning meeting—a tedious affair made only slightly more bearable by the presence of strong coffee and the surprise arrival of a whole box of fresh pastries to mark the fortieth birthday of Frank from accounting—when my eyes found themselves gazing upon Fynn Hartwell, who had paused by the watercooler for a drink. I stopped, pretending to shuffle through some papers while I secretly admired his long, muscular legs inside his sexy black trousers, and his crotch, which sported a wonderful bulge to the soft material. It wasn't the first time he had caught my eye, but this was the best opportunity I'd had yet to properly check him out. Still shuffling my papers, I moved slowly around the side, taking in the view as covertly as I could, until I finally got a good look at his sleek rear as he bent to fill up the plastic cup, my imagination already undressing him and my pulse shifting into a higher gear as I felt my cock stir to life.

"Like what you see?" he asked suddenly, glancing over his shoulder.

"Sorry?" My face reddened as a bolt of alarm shot through me. I struggled to avoid dropping the papers.

"Come on, Adam. You were checking me out," he grinned confidently. "I saw you."

"What?" I blinked, while a little voice deep inside whispered shamefully: *That's sexual harassment in the workplace he's got you for.*

"It's fine, really," Fynn assured me, noting my concern. "I've done it to you, too. Just never knew you felt the same way."

"You've made a mistake," I said quickly, my heart racing, but I knew the beetroot glow of my face had given the game away. But the earth never cracks open and swallows us when we want it to, so I stood there, glowing like a furnace and blinking like an idiot, while my mind raced in circles wondering what to say next.

"Oh?" he moved nearer to me as he stepped away from the cooler. "Then I apologize."

He was so close to me now it was all I could do not to stare. My breath hitched in my throat as he smiled. I had never truly noticed how stunning he was before—dazzling hazel eyes beneath dark tousled hair and just a hint of stubble around his jaw. I realized I should be saying something; instead I was just gaping at him, but my throat and lungs seemed to be having trouble coordinating the words that were colliding in my mind.

"But if I haven't made a mistake," he continued, his voice softening, "you really don't need to worry."

I said nothing, still too busy trying to come up with a reply and noticing all the while how his shirt clung to his upper body in a way that sent fresh shivers of excitement through me. I caught the scent of his aftershave then, and breathed in deeply, wanting to breathe all of him in right then and there. I felt myself hardening fully and grew redder still, knowing my own trousers wouldn't disguise the obvious erection.

And then he was gone, disappearing down the hallway with only a quick glance back. I turned and collided with the water-cooler in my haste to leave, and prayed that nobody had seen anything as I struggled to keep it from tipping over. Flustered and red faced, I slunk back to my office and retreated behind the safety of my desk.

I spent the rest of that day trying, unsuccessfully, to put the whole event out of my mind. But my thoughts kept wandering back to it, haunting me as if the memory were some strange ghost that had set up home in my mind. I shuffled uselessly around the office for the rest of the afternoon, staring at the screen without really seeing it, or flicking idly though paperwork without registering any of the words and figures printed there. Finally when five rolled around, I shut down the computer without remembering to save anything, grabbed my jacket and scarf and hurried out the door, just glad to be outside. Away from those confining walls and the watchful eyes of my coworkers I was finally able to freely turn my attention to the thoughts that had in truth been occupying my mind all day.

It was a cold, crisp evening. January still held the world in an icy grip, and the ground scrunched underfoot with the frost that was starting to form as the dusk gave way to night. I tugged my jacket closer around me as I hurried down the steps alongside the building and out onto the street below. The rush of cars and the fume-filled air greeted my senses as I moved past bright shop fronts that spilled wide strips of light out across the pavement, and made my way to the crowded stop where I caught my bus.

It was a walk I had made hundreds of times before, part of

a routine that rarely varied: same old walk, same old faces in the crowd, even the same graffiti, sprawled in green spray-paint across the top of the bus shelter that read FAREWELL LEMMINGS that nobody had ever bothered to remove. Yet tonight it all felt different.

Sitting on the bus, after I had shuffled onboard with the rest of the lemmings, with the rumbling of the engine forming a steady background noise, I gazed out of the murky window at the condensation-veiled world beyond. The fogging on the windows turned the blurry city lights into coronas of dazzling beauty, making the buildings look like magical towers of some mythical realm against the black of the night.

I imagined myself not on a rattling bus filled with weary commuters but instead on a gilded carriage, being carried through that majestic kingdom. Passing through streets paved with marble and bedecked with bright rainbow flags, on my way to the steps of the palace to meet with a handsome knight, the greatest defender of that fantastical realm.

And there was Fynn, looming in my memory in the role of the knight, striding forward and removing his helmet as the carriage pulled up outside the gleaming steps of the palace. I remembered those sparkling eyes, so full of passion and energy, and his lips, so soft and inviting. And naturally I recalled that wonderful bulge at the front of his crotch that had got me into so much trouble earlier, and began to daydream not about magical kingdoms, but instead about what might be waiting for me behind that enticing veil of cloth.

I've done it to you, too, Fynn's voice echoed through my memory, and I felt a sudden thrill at the recollection and the idea that he had noticed me also.

And then I sat back against the shuddering bus seat, forcing my mind to snap back fully to the reality of the present. Who was I kidding? Even if Fynn really was gay and not just yanking my chain, what could I do about it? There was no way I could come out. I could just imagine the reaction I'd get from my family, and the stronger reaction I'd get from my closest friends if they learned I'd essentially been lying to them all these years. The whole thing had the potential to spiral into a horrible mess. Life was rarely easy. In fact, most of the time it just seemed hideously complicated. So I eased myself down in the seat and tried not to think about any of it, just as I had always done.

When I got into my apartment everything was dark and cold, and I sighed as I reached for the light switch. The boiler must have broken again, for the timer was meant to have started kicking some much needed heat into the place ready for when I got home. I was just on my way to check on it when the phone rang. With a groan of frustration I turned and snatched it off the wall.

"Yes?" I said, more tersely than intended.

"Ouch. Bad day?" my sister's voice piped back at me.

"Oh, Kat. Yeah it's been…"

"Okay, so listen," she continued, cutting me off. "Big news—and you are going to love this. Guess what?"

"I don't know," I replied with audible disinterest. As dear as she was to me, I was in no mood for any of her games tonight. "What?"

"You really are an ogre tonight."

"Been a hell of a day," I explained wearily. "So what's the news?"

"You ready for this?" She waited a beat, then: "Pete proposed to me, right before my birthday too!"

"That's wonderful," I smiled, not telling her that Pete had asked my advice on a ring a month ago. "What a lovely surprise."

"I know!" Her voice had reached almost shrill proportions with excitement, and I found myself wishing, not for the first time, that I had a speakerphone. "So, it's just you now."

"Me?" I frowned.

"To get hooked up with someone. Look, we all know you're lonely. You should get out there, find yourself a good woman. Guy like you shouldn't be alone."

I bit my tongue, rolled my eyes and shifted the phone to my other ear.

"I'm fine, really," I protested, all the while aware of the emptiness of my small apartment, half of it still bathed in shadows and all of it cold.

"Whatever," she said, giving up with an exasperated sigh. "So, are you still coming out on Friday? Restaurant's booked, and I've got two reasons to celebrate now!"

"I don't know." I shook my head, recalling her constant past attempts to hook me up with some new female friend of hers at every given opportunity. She meant well, but it was becoming a regular and excruciating trial to endure, not to mention the effort of having to find a new and believable excuse why I wasn't interested each time.

"It would do you good," she assured me. "And I've got a friend who says she'd love to meet you."

And there it was, as always. The catch.

"I'll think about it," I lied, "but I'll drop your card and present up to you on Wednesday, just in case I can't make it, okay?"

"Oh, okay."

I heard the crushing disappointment in her voice and felt as though someone had just kicked me in the gut. I was a terrible brother, and I knew it. But I couldn't face another painful public charade of pretending I liked women in front of everybody when the truth was I'd much rather be asking out some of the cute waiters around us instead.

By the time I finally got around to checking out the boiler, the house was freezing. I lit a few candles in the faint hope that it might do something to warm the air, but all it got me thinking about was how nice it would be to have somebody to share a candlelit room with, or a sexy guy who knew how to fix boilers at the very least.

I ran into Fynn the next day at work. I had been out in the dusty bowels of the rarely used records department going through some of the old file archives, trying to trace a rogue piece of paperwork that had somehow evaded being properly scanned into the system back when it had come in, when I heard someone approaching. I glanced around to see Fynn watching me, a faint smile playing on his lips as he planted his hands on his hips appraisingly.

"Nice ass," he winked.

I straightened, feeling my face flush once more, but secretly enjoying the attention.

"Figure that makes us even now," he added, moving next to me and leaning against one of the filing cabinets. "Though, I meant what I said—the other day *and* just then."

"Did you?" I asked, my pulse quickening.

"Every word."

I hesitated for a second, and then before I really knew what I was doing I took a step toward him, my eyes meeting his and studying them closely, as though trying to discern whether this was all an elaborate deception or some cruel office prank.

"What are you doing back here?" I asked, knowing how rarely anyone had to access the old files. It wasn't part of the building that saw a lot of visitors.

"Heard you were stuck out here, having to go through all

these," he gestured at the long rows of filing cabinets. "Figured I'd come rescue you from all that tedium. Or at least try to sweeten the time."

His smile was infectious, and more than that, it seemed to be prompting me to levels of bravery I had never expected, for I found myself taking hold of his tie and using it to slowly draw him in closer. "So, what? You're my knight in shining polyester, viscose and cotton?"

"Would that make you a damsel in distress?"

"Don't even go there," I warned jokingly.

His leg was touching mine now and an electric tingle ran through my body. That, combined with the smell of his after-shave, was making it very hard to resist the growing urge to tear off his clothes and have him then and there. A wave of pressure was building within me and the walls I had built up to hide my sexuality from the outside world were crashing down before it. He leaned in, lips almost touching mine.

"Someone could walk in at any time," I whispered, but somehow that just made it more thrilling, and I could see the same excitement burning in his eyes.

"How about we go someplace else, then? After work?"

"I want to, but…" I faltered, suddenly letting go of his tie as a wave of self-doubt flared within me. What the hell was I doing?

"What's wrong?" he frowned. "Something I said?"

"No," I stepped away, shaking my head. The truth was I was as confused and annoyed with myself right now as he must have been. "It's not that."

"Then, what?"

"I don't know if I can."

"But you want to—that's pretty obvious," he said gently. "And you know I like you."

"I know, but…" I trailed off, unsure of how to explain the wave of emotions that were suddenly coursing through me. It seemed I didn't have to, he must have read the expression on my face correctly.

"What are you scared of?" he asked, his eyes meeting mine once more. He reached out and took my hands in his, and at the touch of his skin against mine I wanted to melt into his arms. But still I held back.

"I'm not out yet," I said quietly, wondering if it sounded as pathetic to him as it did to me. "You know what it's like, if people start talking soon everyone knows."

"Would that be so bad?"

"Yes—no… I don't know."

He could have been really pissed off with me then, and I wouldn't have blamed him one bit. In fact I would have sided with him all the way. He could easily and furiously have pointed out that I had been the one to attract his attention, and had only done that because I was very interested, and on some level wanted what I had started. Instead he disarmed me with a kind and gentle smile, and I knew right away when I saw it that his words had been no office prank.

"Are you going to let fear rule you?"

I shook my head, unable to answer as uncertainty coursed through me. As much as I wanted to be free, there was a sense of safety in hiding that I had grown too used to. I knew all too well that once the genie was out of the closet, to adapt a phrase, there was no way of putting it back.

"You can't be happy pretending you're not who you are, living with a whole chunk of yourself locked away in the dark. Denying it won't bring you anything but loneliness. You deserve better than that."

"I've coped this far."

"But are you really happy?"

I didn't reply. I knew he'd see the lie for what it was.

"I thought not," he answered for me. "You said I was a knight; well, your fear is like a dragon, and it's got you imprisoned. If memory serves, knights are meant to slay dragons. So let me help you with that."

"You hardly know me," I said, looking into his eyes again.

"I'd like to change that."

"You might not like what you find," I warned.

"That's always part of the journey. Maybe we find nothing, or we find something that lasts a moment then dies—or maybe we find more, something deeper and stronger. Who can say? Isn't it worth finding out?"

I stayed silent, staring down at the floor, unable to meet his gaze any longer. What he said had resonated deeply with me, and yet still I was afraid of what might happen. I knew if I stepped through that door, I couldn't close it again—and despite all the great strides that the gay community had taken in earning some of the recognition, equality and respect they deserved, I knew that homophobia still lurked like a predator in corners of our society. Was I ready to face that? Was I ready to stand up and be counted, to lose the sanctuary that had kept me hidden and safe for so long?

"If you change your mind," Fynn said, gently releasing my hands as he turned and walked toward the door, "you know where to find me. But I can't wait forever."

I wanted to call out for him to stop. Heck, part of me wanted to grab his arm and keep him there in the room with me. Instead I let him go, but I spent a long time watching that doorway after he had walked through it.

I never did find that paperwork.

Once again I found myself plodding through a day that

seemed to have slowed to an interminable crawl, while struggling to focus on my work. I sat in my chair and stared at my
screen without seeing it and all but ignored my phone. Emails
came in and went unread, and finally the only way my colleagues
could get answers from me was to poke their heads around the
office door and ask in person.

The thing that truly cut deep was that I knew Fynn was right.
I was lonely, and I did want more—but there was a dragon
barring my path, just as he had said, and I didn't know how
to get past it. I had let fear be my master for so long, I didn't
know how to begin to tackle it. I was also keenly aware that
the idea of sex held a curious mixed attraction for me. On the
one hand I wanted it like any horny gay guy did. The magazines and DVDs I had in a drawer at home could attest to that,
as could my right hand. But perversely I was also aware that I
was somewhat intimidated by it. Most guys my age were experienced—and knew just how to hit the right notes and achieve
the desired ends. But not me. My stint in hiding meant I had
only imagination to draw upon, not any actual experience. And
on top of all that, I had to admit I was worried about whether
I would match up in the downstairs department, having had no
real basis for comparison. That didn't help to boost my confidence. But thinking of Fynn—his gorgeous face and sexy body,
the way he had touched my hands and the look in his eyes as he
spoke to me—had set off an avalanche of feelings within me that
was gathering momentum, and the longer I sat there, the more
I knew I had to do something to break through the barriers of
fear that were holding me back before he slipped out of my life.

His office was at the other end of the building, but unlike me
he shared it with four other people, hardly private enough for a
conversation, so instead I opened up an email and typed: *You're
right. Let's slay that dragon.*

SIMON BLEAKEN

It took less than a minute to get a reply back from him. Had he been sitting waiting for me to make contact? He typed: *Glad to hear it. How about going for a drink tonight after work?*

My heart both soared and sank at the same time.

I'd love to. But I've got someone coming to fix my boiler tonight.

I hit SEND, wondering whether it sounded like a really bad double entendre.

This time it seemed to take an eternity for him to reply, though it could only have been a minute. I sat watching my inbox, heart racing with anticipation and dread, until finally his reply appeared: *Why not come over to my place after that?*

My heart leaped into my throat and I felt an uneasy flutter in my stomach as I typed back: *I'd love to.* It took me three attempts to type even those few words properly; my fingers kept tripping over themselves.

He sent me his address, and I agreed to be there around eight thirty. The rest of the day seemed to pass in a daze as I waited for the clock to crawl to five. I rushed out the door before my computer had even finished powering down. I took the steps two at a time in my haste to get to the bus stop. But ironically, everything suddenly seemed to be taking longer—the queue for the bus looked at least twice as busy as usual, and the bus itself only appeared after what felt like a small eternity. And was it me, or was the rush-hour traffic busier than ever before?

I got home—greeted by the usual shadows and chills as I kicked the door shut—only to see a light flashing on the answer phone. With a flurry of panic I wondered if Fynn had called to cancel, and I pressed the button with some unease. My heart lifted at the sound of the repairman apologizing profusely that he wasn't going to be able to make it that night, but would arrange to come back very soon. It was the first time ever that

13

a cancellation like that brought a smile of joy and not a cry of frustration—even if it meant living in a cold apartment for a few days more.

I changed out of my office attire into something more casual and hurried out to the bus stop after grabbing only a very quick bite to eat. My stomach didn't seem to be in the mood for food right now. But by the time I was drawing up at the stop close to Fynn's house—a full hour early, the nerves had started to stir deep within me once more.

When he opened the door I caught my first look at him in casual clothes—a light cotton shirt over a white T-shirt and a pair of dark blue 501s that followed the curves and shape of his legs like a sculpture in denim.

"You're early," he smiled, as his eyes traveled down my body, taking all of me in.

"Is that all right?" I asked. "The boiler guy canceled."

"Sure," he laughed, gesturing for me to enter. "Can I get you a drink, or something to eat?"

We sat for a while talking and laughing over a bottle of wine, getting to know each other better and breaking the remains of any ice that might have lingered, including the all important questions about our health status, both clear. But an unspoken sexual tension was building in the air between us and in the lingering glances we shared, and it didn't take long for us to both feel its pull.

"I want you," he said simply, setting his wineglass down. "I've been thinking about you all day."

"Me too," I admitted. "Since the watercooler, actually."

Fynn rose to his feet, took my hand in his and led me upstairs without another word.

We paused once on the landing to exchange a kiss, and I tasted the wine on his lips as I felt his arms about me. He smiled sheepishly as we entered his bedroom together, my eyes taking in the crumpled bedclothes still thrown aside from that morning, the socks, underwear and a pair of jeans scattered haphazardly on the floor, and a dog-eared copy of *Giovanni's Room* resting on the bedside table. I couldn't help but smile at that, though I hoped it wasn't to prove an omen of things to come.

"Sorry. Haven't got around to tidying yet," he admitted, as though it wasn't obvious. "You surprised me tonight, arriving early. It's not usually like this."

"Course not," I nodded good-naturedly, not believing a word of it. But I was glad for the smile that crossed my face, for it helped me hide the chaotic jangle of nerves that were clattering around inside me. If that feeling had a sound, it would be like the whole brass section of an orchestra slowly sliding off the stage and into a heap. Any little distraction from that feeling helped, but I could still feel a lump in my throat and a curious tingle that seemed to be spreading between my legs. I swallowed and sat down, perching on the side of the bed, keenly aware of the now obviously growing bulge at the front of my tight-fitting khaki cargo pants. I never expected to feel so awkward or vulnerable. In the movies there always seemed to be soft lighting, candles—and frequently the crooning tones of Barry White to stir up the magic. I suppose I shouldn't have been surprised to find that once again reality and Hollywood fantasy rarely mixed.

"Don't be nervous," he whispered, watching me slowly. He moved closer, putting his hands softly on my thighs, running them gently over the material and finally playing with the buttons on the pockets on my legs. "Is this your first time?"

"Yeah," I nodded.

"Don't worry, I'll go slow."

The bulge between my legs was now straining against the

cloth as though trying to burst through, and a dark round spot of precum stained the material to the right of my crotch.

"Someone's happy," he grinned, and leaning over he began to lick and suck at the stain, before turning his lips and tongue to play with the bulge that was still growing inside my trousers. A shiver ran through me, and as he eased me back onto the bed I saw a similar bulge straining against the tight cloth of his jeans. I reached out for him, squeezing and massaging his erect cock through the denim, feeling its warmth and firmness, and then his lips found mine as he slid on top of me, our crotches whispering together as cloth brushed cloth and bulge brushed bulge.

"Lie still," he whispered, nipping my earlobe lightly with his teeth, while his hands reached down and unbuckled my belt. His agile fingers then got to work on the buttons at my crotch, opening them one by one, before sliding my cargo pants down and off and doing the same with my underwear. I shivered and swallowed as my exposed dick brushed against the front of his jeans, leaving a further trail of precum on the dark denim.

"Very happy," he smiled again, looking down at what he had uncovered.

A shiver of doubt awoke within me then, like a dying ember struggling to flare to life one final time. "Is it," I whispered, half afraid to ask, "okay?"

"No complaints so far," he laughed.

The doubt flickered and died, and I lay back, finally allowing myself to relax and enjoy the moment.

He quickly shed his own clothes, kicking them aside, and I caught sight of his cock. It was thin and long and stood proudly up from a tuft of dark pubic hair.

"Do you like what you see?" he winked.

"Oh yeah," I nodded.

He lay next to me and tugged my T-shirt up and over my

head, throwing it onto the floor before playing the tip of his tongue around my nipples and gently running his hands along my chest. I could feel his dick rubbing against my leg, and my own strained in response.

"Is that nice?" he asked softly as he lifted his head, and it was all I could do to nod. The lump in my throat appeared to have blocked off everything but my breathing—and I only did that when I realized I hadn't been. His fingers gently explored my skin, running softly across my chest, getting lower all the time. I felt relaxed and tense at the same time—enjoying the experience and yet waiting anxiously for the moment when I knew he would…

Fynn slid his fingers gently over my balls and up the shaft of my penis, stroking the side of the head and playing with the slit at the top. Again my breath caught in my throat as a wave of pleasure surged through me. Time felt like it had become suspended in amber—seconds seeming to draw out into an eternity, and I didn't want the moment to end.

Then Fynn moved farther down and slipped the head of my dick into his mouth, sucking and running his tongue over the tip as he closed his eyes, and a fresh shiver of delight surged through me. I could feel the pressure building up within me and knew any second I would feel that familiar tingle right before I came. I grasped the bedclothes in my hands, twisting the cloth as I bit my lower lip.

A pleasured grunt escaped my lips as I felt the awaited tingle surge along my swollen shaft—and felt myself come in a wonderful shuddering spasm. I opened my eyes to see Fynn smiling at me, my seed on his lips. And then it was my turn, as Fynn lay beside me and I took the head of his penis into my mouth, repeating what he had done to me, learning from him and feeling the heat of his passion and the throbbing of his erect cock. I took him into my mouth greedily, lips and tongue playing against flesh, delighting in every new experience.

When he too had come, filling my mouth with his shot, he wrapped his arms around me and we rolled back. The frantic passion of my initiation spent, now we just enjoyed the warmth of our bodies as they pressed together, skin against skin. I closed my eyes as he buried his mouth in my neck, planting deep slow kisses from my shoulder to my ear and back again.

I kissed him back, tasting the salty sweat on his body.

"Thank you, sir knight," I whispered, resting my head on his chest.

"Anytime, my prince," he answered.

"I think we killed that dragon."

"Oh yeah," he laughed. "We kicked its ass."

We stayed together like that for the rest of the night.

The first night together was just a tiny taste of the many pleasures that Fynn had in store for me, both in the bedroom and as a companion at my side, as he showed me a side of life I had only dreamed of, and one that was more beautiful and bittersweet with ups and downs than I could have ever imagined, but that I would not have changed for the world.

It has been said that modern society has lost many of its initiation rites for men—those markers and rituals that delineate the different stages of life and growth, such as those found in the ancient and tribal societies from which we have evolved. I think there's a lot of truth in that. But that night, and with my subsequent coming out, I truly shed my old life in my own initiation rite, and embraced a newfound freedom I had never imagined possible.

My friends, all but one, welcomed and accepted my announcement with more support than I had ever expected. Even my sister seemed thrilled for me, and I realized the foolishness of having lived at the mercy of fear for as long as I had. And Fynn was by my side throughout my coming out, his hand in mine—both student and teacher at the same time, helping me take those first steps like a child learning to walk and discovering the true value of the freedom that it brings.

And so, just as true transitions of glass always do, it had come unseen and unexpected, sweeping me into a new stage of my life. One from which I have never looked back.

And if we could have hung that dragon's skull on a wall like a trophy, we would have.

TO DYE FOR

Jay Mandal

Definitely dyed. But cute, nevertheless. I'd always liked blonds, even bottle blonds. "Hi. Can I buy you a drink?"

The look. Assessing. Is this some homicidal maniac or, worse, a bore? The smile. I'd passed the test. "Bacardi Breezer, please."

I got the drinks, and brought them over to the table. "Trevor," I said.

"Sam. Cheers."

"I haven't seen you here before."

"D'you come here often, then?"

We laughed at our attempts at conversation.

"I like your hair," I told him.

"Oh."

"It's all right. I know it's not natural."

"Don't I know you from somewhere? Got it! The King Edward the Sixth Grammar School."

"You went there, too?" I asked.

"No. You got off the bus I used to get on."

"I'm sorry, I don't remem—"

"That's okay. You were a sixth-former. I'd just started at Bash Street School." He meant Bashir Street High. "My friend Sarah Smithers had a crush on you all year."

"How about you?"

"I was a late developer. I was thirteen before I fell in love with Callum Hayward."

"Callum Hayward? Wasn't he expelled for bullying?"

"Yes. I was into masochism at the time. Knocked that on the head I'm pleased to say. I used to think you were *sooo* lucky."

"Why's that?"

"Because you went to an all-boys school."

"We didn't have any time for flirting. The teachers kept us hard at it."

"That's not a double entendre, is it?" Sam asked.

I grinned back. "Wasn't supposed to be."

"So come on: who did you have a crush on? There must have been someone."

"Oddly enough, most of the other boys were straight."

"Shame! Still, that means some weren't. What about those?"

"I was too terrified to talk to them. I was afraid of guilt by association. I pursued a straight-looking and straight-acting policy."

"So what are you doing here?"

"I'm out now. How about you?"

"Guess! Not that I ever had much choice. I always stuck out a mile. So what's a straight boy like you want with a gay guy like me?"

"Straight-*looking*," I corrected.

"Well, you're obviously no longer afraid of guilt by association, but would you introduce me to your parents?"

"Oh, Sam, this is so sudden!" I lisped.

"You owe me another Bacardi Breezer for that."

"You want me to get you drunk?"

"Drunk, sober...can anyone tell the difference?"

I got to my feet.

"Where are you going?"

"To get you another drink."

"I was joking."

"So was I." I sat down again. "What would you like to do this evening, then?"

"I suppose mad, passionate sex is out of the question?"

"Anyone particular in mind?"

"Nah... The crowd in here tonight's pretty naff."

"It is, isn't it?"

Sam grinned. "Besides, I don't. Not on a first date."

"Who said this was a first date?"

"You mean it would be okay?" He looked thoughtful. "I don't know. Do you believe in love at first sight?"

"Oh, Trevor, this is so sudden!"

"I've always liked blonds."

"What if I ran out of peroxide, though? Imagine: you go to bed one night with the love of your life, and the next morning you wake up next to your worst nightmare."

"Why do you dye your hair?" I asked.

"Well, you know what they say."

"Blonds have more fun?"

He sighed. "You're the first person to speak to me all evening."

"Is that good or bad?"

"Is that a trick question?"

"Wasn't supposed to be," I said again. "So is it my dazzling repartee that's getting you down?"

"It's not you—it's me. What word inevitably precedes 'blond'? I'll tell you. The D-word. Dumb. Dizzy. Dippy. Maybe even ditzy, if I knew what it meant."

"But–" I stopped.

"What?"

"I thought that was part of it. Why you wanted to be a blond. You dye your hair to match your personality."

"Dumb, you mean?"

"No. Bubbly. Fun. Outgoing."

"And that's what you want?"

I frowned.

"You said you liked blonds," he reminded me.

"I must remember never to speak the truth again. It can get you into all sorts of trouble."

"What was your previous boyfriend like?"

"Guess."

"Another blond."

I thought about Alec. Definitely not blond or with any of the word's associations. "He was dark."

"How long were you together?"

"Four years."

"So it was serious?"

"Very serious."

Sam looked at me over the top of his glass. "You're on the rebound, aren't you? Just my luck. I find someone—"

"Yes?"

"Someone," he said, refusing to be drawn, "and he's unavailable."

"We split up two years ago."

"But I'm the first—"

"No," I said, just as firmly.

"You're a serial dater, then. Or you're still carrying a torch for him. Or you can't handle commitment."

"I think that's covered every possibility."

"Sorry if I sounded rude. There was a bit of a contretemps at work today."

"A contretemps, eh?"

"Mmm. It's made me more jaundiced than usual. Do I mean jaundiced?"

"I know what you mean."

"It'll be all right as long as I cut down on the carrots."

"If I tell you about my love life, will you tell me about your bad day at the office?"

"Only if you want to tell me. I don't mean to pry."

It was my turn to sigh. "It was very serious between Alec and me. Too serious. We were dragging each other down. All the fun had gone. Each of us knew what the other was going to say. It had become boring. We both wanted out, but neither of us was brave enough to say so. Until one day when we were talking about holidays. Alec had brought home a pile of brochures for me to look at. 'Why don't we go skiing this year?' I said. 'But we always go to the Greek Islands,' he objected. 'So let's do something different.' You'd have thought I'd suggested running naked through the town center. 'I thought you liked beach holidays.' I said I did. Then he said this wasn't really about holidays, was it? And that's when it all came out. All the pent-up feelings and resentments. It finished with us deciding not only that we didn't want to go on holiday with each other, but also that we didn't want to continue living together. Alec was in tears, and I was pretty close.

"So we divided up our possessions, went back to our respective parents while the flat was being sold and then eventually each of us moved into his own place. It was very civilized and very painful." I stopped. For a while, neither of us spoke.

Then Sam said, "I'm sorry."

"Thanks. I'm over it now." I took a sip of my Coke.

"Puts my love life in perspective."

"Oh?"

"Nothing much. Just a trail of boyfriends. Lots of broken hearts, or so I thought at the time, but in retrospect I don't think I've really missed any of them very much. Oh no!"

"What?"

"I sound like a commitment-phobe. Or a perfectionist."

"Not if they broke your heart."

"I broke a few hearts along the way, too."

"I'm sure you did." I finished off my drink.

"Can I get you another?" Sam asked.

"Please." I watched as he wiggled over to the bar. He looked good in jeans. "Nice—of you to get the drinks," I said when he returned, although I had been about to comment on his rear end.

He must have guessed, as he said, "People say it's my best asset—give or take a couple of letters."

We grinned at each other.

"What's yours?" he asked.

I raised my glass. "I haven't finished this one yet. My best asset? A physical attribute or a mental one?"

"Both," he said promptly. "But let's do the physical one first. So much more interesting."

I whispered in his ear.

"God!" he said, his eyes wide. Then they narrowed in suspicion. "How d'you know?"

"It's only an estimate. But I've been told it's…unusual."

"By whom?"

"Let's just say I've had it on good authority."

"Is that another double entendre?"

"My ex."

"Don't you think he might have had an axe to grind?"

"I'm sure he did."

"Or maybe he was just flattering you."

"There've been others. It was commented on at school."

"By the boys?"

"And the teachers."

He spluttered into his drink. "*The teachers?* You were having an affair with one of the *teachers?*"

"Of course not. I just overheard them talking about it one day."

"How does something like that come up in the conversation?"

I leered at him.

"I'll rephrase that. Why on earth were they even talking about your appendage?"

"Well, I'd always taken a towel into the showers with me, even though most of the others hadn't bothered since they were fourteen or so. There was this one boy, Marcus, who delighted in annoying everyone. On this particular day, it was my turn to bear the brunt of his wit. 'What are you hiding, Price? There's no need to be shy—we've all got one.' 'Come on, then, Price, let's see what you've got.' I clung on to my towel. I can be very stubborn when I want to be. So he turned his attention to Robert.

"Robert was a much easier target. Even the teachers picked on him. The poor kid was already whimpering, so I twisted my towel and began to hit Marcus on the legs. Which is when the PE teacher came into the changing room.

"The other boys said Marcus started it.

"'Is this true?' Mr. Atkinson asked me.

"'Yes, sir,' I said. 'Marcus wanted to see my penis. I can

only assume he's gay.' Around me, there were gasps and giggles. Marcus went bright red.

"'I wasn't unduly upset, but then he started on Robert who was clearly not enjoying his attentions.'

"Mr. Atkinson goggled at me. 'Right,' he said eventually. 'Everyone hurry up and get dressed.'

"Later that day, I had to go to the staff room. Mr. Atkinson was talking about the incident. 'He'll make some girl very happy,' he finished.

"*I doubt that very much*, I thought to myself."

Sam looked stunned. "Do you have any personality flaws?" he said eventually.

"I'm too modest."

We burst out laughing.

"Have I cheered you up?" I asked.

"Was it true? All that about school?"

"You'll just have to take it on trust for the time being."

He spluttered into his drink again. "You are seriously—"

"Funny?"

"Rude."

"Oh."

"But you have cheered me up."

"Want to tell me about it?"

He indicated his hair. "It didn't go down well at work."

"What do you do?"

"I work for the Inland Revenue."

"Oh my god! You're one of *them!*"

"I sort of figured you knew that."

We both grinned.

"What's your best trait?" I asked Sam.

"I never hold a grudge. Not against Callum Hayward who held my head down the toilet. Or against Mr. Stapleton who thought it was me that had written something obscene on the blackboard. Or against—"

"I get the message."

"I've forgiven them all," he said nobly.

"Would you like another drink?"

"I'm awash. Any more, and I'd be letting you have your evil way with me."

I stood up as if I was off to the bar again. Then I sat down. "Can I give you a lift home, then?"

He looked like a little boy lost.

"What's wrong?" I asked.

"I think I'm falling in love."

"That's a good thing, isn't it?"

"Is it?"

"I think so," I said gently.

I drove. Sam played with the radio.

When we reached his house, I walked up the path with him, and kissed him on the forehead.

"Oh."

"What's the matter?"

"That's it, is it? I sort of hoped…"

"I thought you said you didn't on a first date."

"It's a lady's prerogative to change her mind." He held the door open for me.

"Looks like you're going to find out if I was joking about what happened at school," I said.

"You'd better not have been."

"Would it make a difference?"

Sam smiled. "Come inside."

So that's what I did.

DISCODEMIUS

Jerry L. Wheeler

"Where are your *claws*, man?" Kevin asked with disappointment once the smoke had cleared. "And your horns—I don't see
any *horns*."

The demon sighed and bent his head forward, parting
his blond, feathered shag haircut to reveal two nubby horns.
"Happy?" he asked. He straightened up and adjusted the collar
of his hot-pink leisure suit jacket. His paisley-patterned Quiana
shirt was open to the waist, revealing a mass of medallions on
gold chains that clacked against his scaly chest.

"No, I'm *not* happy. You don't look like Azmodeus," he
said, pointing to the Wikipedia article displayed on his laptop.
"That's who I called up."

The demon edged to the perimeter of the circle, grazing the
border with the toe of his platform shoe. "I can't quite see it
from here. Maybe you could just erase a little of this circle so I
can come closer."

"I don't think so, man. As long as the circle's intact, you can't get out of it and you can't hurt me. I read up on this shit before I conjured you."

"Hmph," the demon sniffed. "I guess you didn't get to the part that said that's just an artist's rendering. He doesn't photograph well."

Kevin raised his middle finger in triumph. "*Hah!*" he said. "So you're *not* Azmodeus."

"He's at his nephew's bar mitzvah. I'm the on-call demon today."

"Great. Thirty dollars in candles, two hours of chalking weird-ass symbols around this circle and a half-hour of chanting just for the on-call guy. What's your name?"

"I am the unholy terror from the seventies, Discodemius."

Kevin giggled at first, but then he laughed louder and louder until he finally doubled over in mirth, the demon growing angrier by the second. His lizard-lidded eyes narrowed to yellow slits and his dry, crusted lips began to curl with impatience. His foul breath grew rapid and shallow, raising a noxious cloud. He grew larger and larger until the top of his head grazed the ceiling.

"Do *not* mock me!" the demon intoned in a dark, threatening voice that was a multitude of voices. Steam issued from his mouth and nostrils, gathering around the light fixtures like a sulfuric sauna bath as it blistered and peeled the wallpaper. Kevin's laughter subsided to a grin as the demon shrank down to his normal size.

"Heeeeey, that's not bad," Kevin said, "but it'd be scarier if you lost the pink polyester."

"Do I tell *you* how to dress, asswipe? Just give me your Command so I can get back to my dinner."

"Command?"

"Yes, your Command. Your order. What you want me to do.

I thought you said you read up on this."

"Um…yeah, I did."

"No, you didn't—goddammit, I *hate* amateurs. Now you'll have to scramble for something and it's going to be ill-advised or just plain stupid. You really shouldn't call up demons unless you know what you're doing."

Kevin scratched his sparse goatee. "Okay—entertain me."

"Do what?"

"I'm bored. Entertain me."

"Enter*tain* you? What am I, the fucking Village People?"

"Who?"

"Never mind."

"Look, that's my Command. Deal."

The demon's initial scowl turned into an ugly, sardonic grin. He got as close to the edge of the circle as he dared. "Are you *sure?*" he purred—as only a demon can purr.

Kevin no longer looked sure. He did, however, look determined to follow through regardless of the consequences. He shifted his weight to one leg, as he crossed his hairless, sleeve-tatted arms over his narrow chest, obscuring the Abercrombie & Fitch logo on the T-shirt he wore. "Yeah. Do it."

"Very well. Close your eyes."

"Close my eyes?"

"English not your native language? Close your eyes, then open them again."

"Why?"

"Because I'm the demon here and I said to close your eyes and open them again. Jesus *Christ*, you're tough to work with."

Kevin closed his eyes for only a second, then opened them again quickly. But that long blink was all the demon needed. Kevin's entire apartment was empty—no furniture, no posters, no laptop and no throw rugs. And he stood in the middle of this empty room totally naked. "What the fuck did you do with all my stuff? And my *clothes*?"

The demon smiled. "Technically, nothing. They still exist—just not in nineteen seventy-four. Most of your stuff hasn't been invented yet. As you can see, I've also removed your tattoos. That should make it easier for you in some ways. However, I've let you keep the earring. At least people will know you're gay."

"How did you know I was gay?"

"Please. A thin, hairless twink with ink, a Tintin haircut, an earring, an A&F T-shirt and skinny jeans. That flame can be seen from space." His eyes went to Kevin's nether regions. "However, you do have some positive attributes. That cock ought to make you pretty popular at St. Mark's—maybe get you a couple meals or a few nights in a warm bed with some sugar daddy."

"Wait, you said 1974—it's 1974 *now*?"

"I thought it'd be 1975 before you caught on. We're still in New York City, though. I've taken you back in time, leaving you stranded with no clothes, no money, no possessions and no way to get back to 2012. Are you entertained yet?"

"How long do I have to stay here?"

The demon shrugged again. "Time is a pretty relative concept. Let's see. I need to finish dinner, help the kids with their homework, then there's that hentai tentacle erotica I TIVO'd—that always gets the old lady worked up—hit the sack early… mmmmm…how about…as long as I fuckin' *want* you to stay here? That work for you?"

"Not exactly," Kevin replied, a sudden sad look in his eye once again replaced by bluster. "Maybe I'll look up Bill Gates or Steve Jobs. Give 'em some ideas, you know?"

"And do you know how to find these entrepreneurs?"

"Well, no."

"Why don't you *Google* 'em?" the demon laughed, vanishing

in a cloud of smoke nearly as thick as the one he'd arrived in.

Kevin rolled his eyes. "Asshole."

Without the demon around, Kevin's veneer of bravado vanished as completely as his clothes. He started to sink down on the bare wooden floor but stopped when he noticed how dusty it was. *Am I that bad a housekeeper?* he wondered. The floor was no cleaner in the corner, but at least he had a wall for support. He padded over, swept the area with the sole of his foot and sat down.

The second his ass hit the cold floor, he heard what sounded like a cash register in the apartment next door, followed by a thudding bass. He swung his arm around to pound on the wall, but then thought of his next-door neighbor Mrs. Mancuso. *That has to be her,* he thought. *She's lived there like, forever.* He couldn't remember ever hearing music coming from her apartment, though; only the wonderful smell of marinara sauce and yeasty Italian bread. Kevin's stomach rumbled.

She's cool, he thought. *She'll listen to me. Maybe even lend me a robe.* Of course meeting someone when totally naked is always difficult, but these things can't be helped. He stood up and took one more look around the apartment for a towel or a sheet, but the place was bare. *Fucker's thorough,* he thought. He put on his winning smile along with his most sincere look—which was all he *could* put on—and opened the apartment door.

The hallway was empty. Oddly enough, it looked nearly the same as it did in 2012. The royal-blue carpet was a bit less threadbare, but not much. Cobwebs still moored the ornate wall sconces just above reach, but they were now rooted in fussy, pansy-cluttered wallpaper instead of chipped pastel blue paint. Either way, they didn't throw enough light to reach the locks in the doors.

Kevin stepped out of the apartment, making sure the door was unlocked before it closed behind him in case he needed to beat a hasty retreat. He listened at Mrs. Mancuso's door for a few seconds, hearing a ripping sax solo coming from inside. He knocked, suddenly feeling very naked—the possibility of being seen was also giving him a semi. Kevin heard shuffling from inside, then noticed the smell of weed. *Mrs. Mancuso smokes dope?*

The door opened, but Mrs. Mancuso wasn't behind it. Kevin found himself staring into the violet-blue eyes of a guy about his own age. His shoulder-length brown hair was freshly washed— still damp, in fact—and he wore a tight, faded pair of 501s with no shirt. A mat of hair encircled his large nipples, spanning his chest and tapering down to a treasure trail that dipped enticingly south. The towel draped over his shoulder fell to the floor as he smiled and extended his hand out to Kevin.

"Hey, howyadoin'? Mikey said he was sending someone over to help, but he didn't tell me he'd be this cute. Or this naked. C'mon in." Kevin followed him inside and shut the door, unable to keep his eyes off the way the Levi's hugged the guy's ass. "Name's Mark."

"I'm Kevin."

"So, what happened to your clothes? No, wait, don't tell me. You stopped at a trick's place on the way over and something happened. Maybe his old lady came home, and he hustled you out the back door before you could get dressed, right?"

"Something like that."

"Fucker. I'm surprised the pigs didn't pick you up. You must know some back alley routes. I got some jeans and a T-shirt you can borrow," he said, looking back with a grin as he sauntered into the bedroom, "but I kinda like you this way."

Kevin took a look around the room. Braided oval throw rugs were scattered on the floor along with cardboard squares, boards and cans of paint. Two vinyl beanbag chairs flanked the large picture window overlooking the park, and beneath the window was a stereo resting on long planks held up by cinder blocks. A marred and scarred coffee table held a bag of pot, a few clay pipes and a bong along with a lighter and a fuming stick of incense.

The sax solo faded into a wash of organ and a loping beat as Mark returned with a T-shirt for himself and some clothes he tossed to Kevin. "Don't get too used to those," he said, smirking. "I have a feeling they're coming off again after we finish the signs." He sat down with his legs crossed under the coffee table and started filling one of the pipes. "Acapulco Gold." he said. "This is some great shit."

"Sure," Kevin replied. He stepped into the jeans, discarded the T-shirt and sat down beside Mark, their legs touching beneath the table.

"You like Pink Floyd?"

"Who?"

"No, Pink Floyd." Mark gestured toward the stereo with the pipe. "*Dark Side of the Moon.* Best album ever made for fucking." He lit the pipe and hit it, handing it over and letting his fingers linger on Kevin's.

Kevin smiled as he took a quick hit, breathed out and took a deeper one. "And you think we're gonna fuck?" He already knew they would, but he didn't want to appear too easy.

Mark grinned. "I was hopin'," he replied. He let out his breath and leaned in for a kiss. Kevin inched closer, putting an arm around Mark's shoulder and drawing him in. The smell of his soap, the slightly bitter taste of pot resin on his lips and the fragrance of the incense all melded, making Kevin a bit dizzy. Mark's lips were soft, and their tongues danced a slow hustle as their hands went to each other's crotches.

Kevin felt his cock stiffening under Mark's touch, but as soon as he firmed up nicely, Mark pulled away and broke the kiss. "Business before pleasure," he said with a smirk. "Why don't you turn the record over, and I'll open up the paint."

"Turn the…"

"…record over," Mark finished for him, "so the first side can play again."

Kevin wasn't stupid—he'd seen records on the Internet and had a vague idea of the process, but he didn't have any actual practice. Did you physically turn it over, or was there a button you pressed somewhere? He moved to grab the edges of the record but was hypnotized by the lazy revolutions of the label, a prism set in a sleek circle of black, tumbling edge over edge into infinity as the play-out groove washed toward it and receded again, a thin line ebbing and flowing, keeping immeasurable time.

"Is the Acapulco Gold gettin' to ya?" Mark asked, laughing as he brushed him aside. "You'd better let me do that—I don't want my album scratched. Can you open the paint?"

"Sure. I don't think paint cans have changed much."

"What?"

"Never mind." Kevin stepped off the oval rug onto the sheet-covered floor and sat down cross-legged in front of the supplies, prying the top off one of the cans of black paint with a spattered chisel. "What are we painting anyway?"

"Signs for tomorrow." A heartbeat, screams and talking filled the room, intensifying until all the sounds peaked, coalescing into a loping mid-tempo bass line. "You know, the Pride march. Didn't Mikey tell you?"

"Oh—um, yeah."

Mark sat down beside him and handed him a placard. "Here—you do 'Gay and Proud' and I'll do 'Closets Are for Clothes.'" They took tokes off the pipe and got to work. Kevin loved Mark's nearly cursive lettering, especially his Os, which were long and thin—more like matched parentheses than letters. His sign looked scrawled in comparison.

Guitars chimed in open, drawn-out chords suspended with fat measures of sustain as Kevin held the brush in midair, watching Mark. His long hair fanned out over his bare shoulders, framing his face and those intense violet eyes, his unshaven scruff looking rugged and masculine. His belly was flat and taut, and Kevin wanted to reach out and rub it but was hesitant to startle him. He felt his cock stiffening again. He extended his big toe and gently nudged the ball of Mark's foot, grazing the warm, hardened skin.

Mark looked up and smiled, edging closer. "You're dripping."

"Huh?"

"You're dripping paint on your sign."

"Oh—sorry."

Mark laughed, a low chuckle that got Kevin even hornier, if that was possible. He took Kevin's brush away and put both of them down on the rim of the paint can. "I can see we're not gonna get anything done until we get this out of the way."

Pink Floyd commanded them to breathe—breathe in the air. And that's just what Kevin did, letting Mark take hold of his hands and pin his arms over his head, laying him back and hovering over him. Soft washes of pedal steel guitar and synths filled the room, encouraging their languid explorations as Mark lowered himself onto Kevin. Their mouths connected again, rougher and less tentative, eager for the next round.

As they kissed, Kevin freed his hands and caressed Mark's furry chest, moving down inside his jeans to graze the oozing tip of his hard cock, drawing a sigh from him. His hand came away slick and wet, and Kevin grinned as he broke their kiss to lick the precum from his fingers. Mark sucked on Kevin's thumb and ground his crotch into Kevin's, their groins wet and hard against each other as the music faded and the sound of running issued from the speakers.

Kevin and Mark matched the urgency of the footfalls echoing around them, pressing harder against each other, their fingers and hands as frantic as the pulsing vocoder line that danced around the steps and the sounds of exertion—tongues, bellies, thighs, bare feet, hairy forearms, shoulders, muscled backs, flashing teeth and hard, jutting nipples—their heavy breathing in tune and as one with the sound effects.

They pushed each other's jeans down, discarding them with careless urgency as the cacophony built, Mark sliding down Kevin's chest to take his hard cock into his mouth. The footsteps got louder and the screams rose around them along with the sound of an airplane spinning out of control, much like Kevin's head dizzied from the pot and the sound and the silken feel of Mark's tongue bobbing up and down frantically on his dick.

Down and down the airplane spun, the sound now all Kevin could hear as Mark caressed his balls. His load of spunk built quickly. Kevin's legs trembled in time with the vibration of the floor and the speakers, shaking even more as Mark pumped his dick and stuck his tongue in Kevin's hole. Kevin shuddered and exploded just as the plane crashed and silence reigned for a moment.

But Pink Floyd wasn't finished and neither was Mark. Kevin heard the faint sounds of a clock ticking as Mark began tickling the hairs in the crack of his ass with his fingers, diving in with his lips and tongue once again to the noise of more clocks and more ticking, as if every antique timepiece in the world was in the room counting down the seconds to orgasm. One alarm clanged, setting off all the others to a maelstrom of ringing as

Mark wet a finger and pushed deeply into Kevin's ass.

Bells clanged as Kevin opened up and Mark settled himself between Kevin's legs, pushing his cock relentlessly in as metronomes kept time and other percussion warmed up an irregular beat until Kevin thought his head might burst. Then suddenly they were all in time and tune, Mark's rhythmic strokes true and ceaseless. The singer shouted about time, Kevin grabbing Mark's hips and thrusting himself into them, pushing Mark's cock deeper inside, pulsing to Mark's short, sharp breaths. The guitar solo screamed, driving Kevin's desire higher and higher as he bucked into Mark.

Mark pounded Kevin with a steady 4/4 beat, sweat beading his forehead as he squinched his eyes and drove it home, his panting chest heaving with lustful exertion. He pulled out and jacked his cock just as the second solo ended, shooting a heavy load all over Kevin's chest, some hitting his mouth.

Kevin laughed and licked greedily, milking his own hard dick for a second load that shot up Mark's back. The guitar and drums faded into a soft piano solo as Mark collapsed onto Kevin's chest, both trying to slow their breathing as Clare Torry's wordless vocals cooed, swooped and swirled around them. "The great gig in the sky," Mark sighed as they cuddled on the floor, kissing softly as they listened to the fadeout.

Then all was silent.

"I don't know about you," Kevin said into Mark's ear, "but I'm ready for Side Two."

"Okay," Mark said to the seven people in his living room. "What did we do right today?"

"We got a total of twenty-one dollars and seventy-two cents in fund contributions," said a girl in a frizzed-out blonde Afro, jeans and an embroidered vest over a denim shirt.

"Good, good—what else?"

"I handed out all seventy-five leaflets," Kevin said proudly, "and fished out thirty-five from the trash barrels around the area. That means at least forty people took theirs home."

"Not counting the hundreds who saw the signs and the people who stopped to talk to us," added a guy wearing a Che Guevara T-shirt, his long, red hair in a braid. "That's good, right?"

"Right," Mark nodded, smiling. "All great. But something I was thinking about today—look at how we're all dressed. Jeans, T-shirts, grubby clothes. We need some people dressed nicer too, so the people see gay men and women of all kinds. Not just our age. We need older people too. People in uniforms, maybe. Black people, brown people, yellow people, all carrying signs." He got up and paced around the room. "The more kinds of gay people we get, the more straights will understand that we're everywhere and everything and everyone."

"Right on," said the girl. "We need more lezzies too."

Everybody chuckled. "We need more of everyone," Mark said with a smile. "Don't get me wrong—today was great. Let's make the next one even better." They began gathering their signs and moving toward the door, some stopping to talk for a moment before leaving.

"Hey you guys," the guy with the big red braid said, approaching Mark and Kevin, "you wanna meet up later?"

"I don't know, Mikey," Mark said. "Kevin and I have something going on right now."

Mikey looked suspiciously at Kevin. "Um...okay. Call me."

"You got it—so long, Mikey."

Mark closed the door on the group, some still talking in the hallway. "He still swears he never sent you that night."

Kevin snaked his arms around his waist and nuzzled his neck. "Mikey's smoked so much dope, I'm surprised he remembers to tie his shoes. You know, I love you when you get all radical like that."

Mark gathered him close. "You love me like you love pepperoni pizza, or you really love me? I mean, you wouldn't say it back to me the other day."

"I told you, it just surprised me, that's all." He snuggled into Mark as they clumsily crossed to the sofa and sat down. "You're the first guy who ever said that to me. I had to think about how I felt. And I *do* love you."

"Good," Mark said as he got up and dug deep into the pocket of his jeans. "Then I won't have to take these back." He produced two small boxes, one of them gift-wrapped.

"Presents?" Kevin asked.

"You don't remember what today is?" he said, handing the wrapped one to Kevin. "It's the two month anniversary of the day you walked—buck naked—into my life. And you stayed. I haven't been the same since."

"I haven't either," Kevin agreed, tearing open his package. He opened it to find a simple silver ring with a murky oval-shaped stone.

"I have a matching one," Mark said, opening the other box. He grasped Kevin's hand, took his ring and placed it on Kevin's middle finger. "Now you do me."

Kevin slipped the other ring on Mark's finger. "Aren't we supposed to say something? Like a vow?"

"That's for straight people," Mark replied with a grin. "Isn't this enough?"

"Yes. Yes, it is—what kind of stone is this?"

"The guy at Bonwit Teller called it a 'mood ring.' It's supposed to change color according to your mood."

"They're kinda blue right now. What's that supposed to mean?"

"Must mean we're happy," Mark replied, drawing Kevin up from the sofa and holding him close. They kissed long and hard, Kevin reaching down to embrace Mark's stiffening dick, but he pulled away. "Now, now," Mark said. "That's for later. Right now we've got dinner reservations at Gallagher's Steakhouse, and then we're going to 12 West for a little disco action. Tonight's all about us, baby."

The steaks were tender and the evening beautiful as they emerged from the subway station and walked the rest of the way to 12 West, laughing and talking as if they'd known each other far longer than two months. "I need some smokes," Mark said. "There's a little grocery store down the block. Hang on. I'll be right back."

Kevin watched him walk away. Even a good half block away from the open door, he could hear the thump of classic disco. *Only it's not classic disco*, he thought. *It's just disco—but it's amazing.* In fact, he was amazed by so much in his new life. There was Mark and the music and the incredible friends he'd made. And there was fighting for a cause. Something to believe in.

Lots of battles have already been won back in 2012, he thought, *but now I'm helping fight them. It's so much better than sitting on your ass in front of a computer liking "social change" on Facebook. I don't miss any of that. I thought I would, but it just doesn't matter anymore. This matters—to everyone.* But then he thought of how HIV would change the landscape in just a few years.

They don't know, he thought. Kevin wished he could warn everybody. He'd save a whole generation of gay men; save their accomplishments, their heart, their music, their art. He could change the face of gay culture but as he felt his heart lifting at the prospect, he knew how impossible that would be. No one would listen. *It sounds so improbable*, he thought. *A gay plague will come and devastate us—sounds like something Anita Bryant would say.*

He saw Mark coming down the block, tapping the pack of cigarettes on his wrist the way he always did, a huge grin spreading across his face as he ran triumphantly toward Kevin. *This is all there is right now*, he thought. *Him and me.* Just as Mark was closing the distance between them, Kevin smelled something like rotten eggs behind him and turned to see a familiar scaly face.

His blond hair was still shag-cut and his horns were still nubby, but he seemed to have more gold chains around his neck. He grinned, revealing uneven rows of stained and broken teeth, and there was no mistaking the gleam in his piss-yellow eyes. He spoke not a word, but held up his wrist and pointed to his Mickey Mouse watch.

And that's when Kevin fainted.

"Are you sure you're gonna be all right?" Mark said, half a cup of coffee in his hand. "You were up most of the night. I can always call in if you feel bad—I mean, that's what they give me time off for. And I wouldn't mind taking care of you."

"I'm fine," Kevin replied. "I was fine last night. I just ate too much. We should have gone in. I still feel bad about ruining our celebration."

Mark shrugged. "We have the rest of our lives to celebrate."

"Would you go to work already?" Kevin said. "I'll call you later, okay?" He took Mark's coffee cup away and kissed him.

"You better."

Kevin looked into his eyes, feeling as if it was the last time he'd ever see him. He held him close and kissed him again, longer and more passionately than he'd ever kissed anyone before. He longed to run away with Mark, to go somewhere where they'd never be found. But that wasn't going to happen.

"Wow," Mark said. "What was that for?"

"Because I love you. Now get outta here."

"Okay. Love you too." He grabbed his jacket out of the closet and went to work, leaving a scent of soap and musk behind for Kevin to smell. He inhaled it even as it melded with the sulfur smell once again.

"Touching," the demon said, standing in the middle of the oval rug. "I could almost cry."

"What are you doing here? I didn't call you."

"I can appear residually from your *last* call."

"What about the circle?"

The demon sighed. "I can't move off this frickin' rug. But I don't need to. Anyway, we're almost finished here. All I have to do is send you back."

"Now? What the fuck? I *like* it here, I have friends, I'm in love and you want to fucking send me back? No way."

"Too bad, sunshine—you don't have much choice. Demon here, remember?"

"I don't *want* to go back."

The demon twisted his neck, looking around. "Sorry. I was trying to find someone who cares."

"Can't we make some kind of deal?"

"Deals. Everybody wants to make a deal. 'I'll give you gold, I'll give you my firstborn, I'll give you my undying loyalty'—yada, yada, yada. I got gold comin' out my ass, undying loyalty's a transient commodity at best and I need another kid like I need a second tail. No deals. You got nothin' I want."

Kevin rubbed his crotch. "Not even..."

"Please, junior. Got more than my share of butt-boys too—and I like 'em with a little more meat on their bones."

"Hey, you don't have to be insulting about it."

"Oooo—touchy. Just blink and it'll all be over with. You'll be back in your snug little place with all your toys."

"I don't want to go." Kevin resisted the urge to blink, then suddenly the landscape around him melted, running down in puddles as it revealed his old apartment. His laptop hummed, his ice-making refrigerator clunked as a few blocks fell into the tray and his smartphone vibrated on the counter.

"And here you are," the demon announced.

"This sucks," Kevin said, tears springing to his eyes. He wiped them away with the hem of his T-shirt. "Can you tell me what happened to him? Where he is?"

"Who?"

"Mark, you fuckhead. My boyfriend."

The demon pursed his lips and fingered one of the ankhs around his neck. "No clue. Couldn't tell you anyway. It's against the rules."

Technological instinct taking over, Kevin ran to his laptop, intent on Googling Mark, but as he approached the dark screen, he didn't recognize his own reflection. His hairline had receded and his jowls were thicker, the skin of his throat slack and hanging. He ran to the bathroom mirror and screamed. "You son of a *bitch*! I'm an old *man*."

"No shit, gramps. Almost forty years have passed."

He ran across the room to rush the demon but smashed against an invisible barrier around the circle of protection. "*I'll rip your fuckin' head off!*" he bellowed, pounding against it.

"Time's kinda tricky that way," the demon said, grinning as he buffed his nails. "I can circumvent the aging process going into the *past*, but not on the way back to the *future*. Odd, isn't it? I let you keep the mood ring and the clothes, though."

Kevin whimpered and slid to the floor, his back against a

wall he couldn't see. He started sobbing. "How much time has passed?"

"In 2012? Oh, about three or four minutes."

"You mean…oh Jesus, what will my *sister* say? My *folks*? I think I'm older than my dad."

"Not my problem, buckwheat. Look, I hate to devastate and run, but I've got other clients. So, just to finish up the formalities, have you been *entertained?*"

"Whaddya mean?"

"That was your original Command. You wanted to be entertained, and the friendly folks at Demon Central want to make sure you're a satisfied customer. So, once again I have to ask, have you been *entertained?*"

"What if I say no?"

"Then I get to stay here and think of even more interesting ways to entertain you. And I can be very creative."

"Yes," Kevin mumbled.

"Yes, what?" the demon said. "It has to be in the form of a statement."

"Yes. I've. Been. Fucking. Entertained."

The demon smiled, rubbing his hands together. "Excellent. Well, the next time you need anything, don't hesitate to call us up. We're here twenty-four seven for your demonic pleasure. Catch you at the next AARP meeting, fucktard."

Discodemius vanished.

And Kevin wept.

His mood ring was black, and he kept twisting it on his finger, taking it off and putting it back on, buffing the stone like some magical genie's lamp that might grant him enough wishes to get back to Mark. He lounged on his sofa, watching the news when he wasn't considering how his newly acquired paunch stretched out his A&F T-shirt. He couldn't fit into his skinny jeans anymore and had to settle for a pair of sweats he borrowed from Mrs. Mancuso. He had to tell her he was Kevin's uncle, in for an unexpected visit. She looked at him like she didn't believe him, but she gave him the sweatpants anyway.

He figured he'd be getting a lot of those looks.

The hair on his arms was gray, the skin thinner and less elastic, and he got winded going upstairs. *Getting old sucks balls*, he thought. *At least it does when it happens all at once. Maybe it's better if it happens gradually. Or not.* He got a twinge in his knee as he swung his legs over the arm of the sofa to lie back and watch TV, staring at his stomach instead. *It looks bigger from this angle, if that's humanly possible.*

He switched his view to the flat-screen, taking in a crowd shot of the Occupy Wall Street protesters in Zuccotti Park. If he turned the sound off and opened the window, he could hear the fracas live, but he preferred the NBC version. Kevin hadn't paid much attention to the whole issue before. It was just an inconvenience for anyone going uptown.

Now, however, he wondered what the hell they were so upset about. He read a few of the signs, but they weren't too issue-specific. But then he saw one that gave him a start. He sat bolt upright, his heart in his mouth. "*GO BACK!!*" he screamed at the screen. And, as if it had been listening, the camera settled on the protester who held it—but Kevin wasn't listening to what he was saying. He was staring at the sign.

The *O* in *Occupy* was long and thin, like matched parentheses. And the rest of it was cursive, not scrawled like everyone else's. *It's one of Mark's signs*, Kevin thought. *It has to be. He's there. He wouldn't be anywhere else.* And as the camera went back to a long shot, Kevin noticed more signs that resembled Mark's. He looked down at his mood ring, which seemed to be glowing a bit bluer.

And then he was off.

He didn't grab his keys or lock his door—just ran down the stairs, hit the door and flew down the sidewalk for about a quarter of a block. Breathing heavily by that time, he had to stop and lean against a building as his heart hammered in his chest. His mouth dry and his thoughts racing, he forced himself down to a fast walk that became a trot when his aching legs would allow, and he soon reached the throng of protesters and police.

He stood on the corner of Liberty and Trinity, deciding to go around to the rear of the crowd, but he was sidetracked by a short blonde woman in a yellow sundress holding one of Mark's signs. "Where did you get that sign?" he asked, not even noticing what it said.

"Oh, isn't it *lovely*?" she cooed. "It really stands out, doesn't it? I got it from some old guy."

"Some old guy? Where is he?"

"A long block down that way," she said, pointing in the opposite direction. "He's making them in the middle of the crowd at a big table—you can't miss it." Kevin didn't even thank her before he started running again, but his progress was slowed by protesters and an advancing line of police with riot gear and shields. He plowed straight into the action, watching for more of Mark's work.

The crowd thickened as Kevin's legs began to throb, but he threaded his way through the mob. *Mark* would *be at the center of this shit*, he thought. Kevin's claustrophobia was beginning to grip him, but he kept his focus on finding Mark despite his shortness of breath and the feeling of panic rooting itself in his brain. He wanted to flail his way above the body of people and get some air, but they compressed him from all sides.

Just as he felt he would faint, he nearly bisected himself on the edge of a long table. Paint cans littered its top, some overturned and some upright, with oozy brushes stuck here and there. And at the opposite end stood a stooped guy about Kevin's new age, wearing faded Levi's and a white T-shirt with his long gray hair tied back, furiously painting a sign as he barked orders.

"Jen, this is the last one. Gather up all the paint you can find and meet me a couple of blocks from Liberty in about an hour. Bob, try to get the table folded up and go with her—if things get hairy and you have to sacrifice it, don't worry. The cops are too close, and there's always tomorrow."

"*MARK!!*" Kevin screamed.

Mark looked up, his violet eyes searching for whoever shouted his name, then they landed on Kevin. He frowned, leaning forward a bit and squinting. He raised a hand to shade his eyes against the glare, then his face widened with recognition. "Omi*god!*" he shouted. "Oh *fuck*. Kevin? *Kevin!*" He tried to go around, but people were jammed against the table, so he climbed on top, kicking cans and brushes out of the way and extending his hand.

Kevin grasped it, grinning at Mark's touch as he climbed up on top of the table with him and they embraced, Mark crying and unintelligibly screaming into Kevin's shoulder. Kevin couldn't hear him or understand him, but he got the gist of it anyway. He grabbed Mark's face and kissed him. "I have to explain some things," he said.

"Not now. I just want you here with me. I didn't ask you any questions when you walked into my life the first time, and I won't now. Just tell me one thing—are you free? Are you still mine?"

"Yes. And yes."

Tears streamed down Mark's cheeks. "Then we can move mountains—c'mon, let's show these kids how fuckin' radicals *used* to do it. Grab my waist and follow my lead."

Kevin grabbed Mark and jumped off the table into the crowd, Mark fighting his way to the front of the line as the police advanced. Kevin could see their shields and helmets mere feet away. "*Link arms!*" Mark screamed to everyone around. "*Link arms!*"

They linked with each other and then to the people on either side, and the linking spread until there was a solid line of men and women.

"*THE WHOLE WORLD IS WATCHING!!*" Kevin shouted, repeating it as the linked men and women picked up the chant. "*THE WHOLE WORLD IS WATCHING!! THE WHOLE WORLD IS WATCHING!!*" As they chanted, the line moved toward the police, but Mark wasn't finished with his instructions.

"*Go down on your knees!!*" he screamed, his voice breaking. "*Crawl toward the fuckers!! Submission is strength!!*" He sank down to the sidewalk, forcing Kevin and the rest of the linked line to do the same, still advancing on the police. The crowd behind the line saw what was happening and also went down on their knees, inching their way slowly toward the riot-equipped police force. "*THE WHOLE WORLD IS WATCHING!! THE WHOLE WORLD IS WATCHING!!*"

Kevin looked over at Mark, his face a reflection of radical ecstasy. He felt no panic, no claustrophobia, no anxiety—just pure and simple love. And they crawled together on the sidewalk, mouths open with unrepentant joy, their hearts beating as one as they received the pepper-spray sacrament.

Five stories above, Discodemius perched on a building ledge between two pigeon-shit coated gargoyles who bore not a little family resemblance. He held a cell phone to one pointed ear, his wings twitching nervously.

"How the fuck was I supposed to know they'd find each other...what am I, psychic or something? Oh...I *am*? Why isn't that in the manual? Oh...it *is*? Look, I took his youth away from him—that's gotta count for something, right? Okay, so he's happy. It's not my *fault*, man. I'm a victim of circumstance... another five hundred *years*? Just for *this*? No way—that's bullshit. I'll file a fuckin' grievance, just you wait!"

He snapped the cell phone shut and slipped it in the pocket of his hot-pink leisure suit jacket. "I *hate* this goddamn job," he said. Glaring at nothing, he spat on the crowd below and pushed off, flapping his leathery wings as he glided into the clouds.

JURY DUTY

Tom Baker

Tim had never been called up for jury duty before, but there it was, the official yellow envelope from the New York State Court System, on the gateleg table in the entryway of his brownstone building on West Tenth Street, along with the Con-Ed bill. *They know where I live,* he thought. Tim opened the envelope even before climbing the three flights of stairs to his apartment. His instructions were to report to the county clerk's office at 100 Centre Street at 8:00 a.m. on February 14, 1975.

What? On Valentine's Day? The notice warned that failure to report would result in a warrant for his arrest.

"Fuck!" Tim said. "Just what I need when I'm trying to get a job." But then, it did pay five dollars a day. "Great. What does that buy at Balducci's? A basket of raspberries."

Tim showed up at 100 Centre Street on Valentine's Day as ordered. The elevator to the fifth floor, filled with prospective jurors, was as big as his apartment. The doors opened, and the crowd poured out to get in line to fulfill their civic duty.

"Take a seat, Mr. Halladay," a bored clerk instructed without looking up at him. "We'll call you." Resigned to going along with the system, Tim sat in the jury assembly room with about a hundred people who didn't want to be there either. He had brought *The New York Times,* which he began to read, section after section, even Sports and Letters to the Editor. After an hour, the doors opened, and the clerk started calling out names.

"Tim Halladay," the clerk called. "In here." Tim followed a line of people down the hall to the jurors' holding room. Another long waiting period ensued in an antiseptic room with fluorescent lighting and hard plastic chairs. After sitting around for another hour, Tim was instructed to go into the courtroom. He had been selected as juror number two, subject to confirmation by the prosecuting and defense attorneys. *Well,* Tim thought. *It's better than sitting in the holding room with nothing to do.*

The jurors took their places in the courtroom jury box. The judge entered the chamber draped in her black robe.

"Is that the judge?" Tim joked with the young woman next to him. She was not amused, obviously taking the whole process very seriously. "Sorry," he said, burying his head in his newspaper.

The judge read off a litany of rules and regulations, saying the attorneys could question any juror to determine if there was reason that any prospective juror should be excused. First step: answer simple questions—place of residence, occupation, any former jury duty. That process over, the prosecuting attorney read an opening statement of the case. The defendant told the police that he had killed his mother-in-law when he mistook her for a raccoon. Hours later his wife had testified that she'd committed the crime. She had confessed to killing her mother in the garage, and that her husband had lied to protect her. She testified that her husband had gone to the garage with her mother to look for a raccoon. An argument took place in the garage resulting in an injury to the older woman. The husband returned to the house screaming that his mother-in-law was hurt and needed help. The wife rushed to the garage and saw her mother lying in a pool of blood on the cement floor. The wife testified that she then picked up a hatchet and repeatedly struck her mother.

The husband told police that he had hit his mother-in-law once when he mistook her for a large raccoon. The mother-in-law weighed 270 pounds. Later he told police that he had hit her in self-defense. The police report showed that the older woman was struck at least eighteen times with a blunt instrument.

The jurors sat frozen in silence. No one had been prepared for such a bizarre case. The husband was on trial for killing his mother-in-law, although his wife had confessed to the killing. This was going to be a tangled case of who did what and why, and of "he said, she said."

The lawyers began questioning the jurors, asking if they had any previous knowledge of this case or knew any of the parties involved. This took several hours. Tim had no knowledge of this incident, and of course did not know anyone involved. The people in the case all lived in Mineola, Long Island. The lawyers also questioned each juror about the death penalty, and asked if they in good conscience could condemn someone to death by execution. The impaneling process ended early in the afternoon, and the judge dismissed the jurors, ordering them back to court at 9:00 a.m. the next day.

The judge then advised, "Because of the sensational aspects of this case and the high media interest, I am ordering that the jury be sequestered for the duration of the trial. If this is a hardship for any of the jurors, please see the bailiff. But also be advised that any request to be excused will be fully scrutinized. Any false information will be dealt with according to the laws of the State of

New York. I would advise you to bring at least three days of clean clothes, because this could go on for some time. The court will provide housing and meals for all the time you are on jury duty. You will be staying at the downtown Sheraton Hotel, but you will not have access to television or newspapers. You may not discuss this case with anyone. Thank you for your patriotic support of the judicial system," she said before leaving the courtroom.

Why do I feel like I'm the one on trial? Tim wondered as he left the courthouse. He opted to walk back to his apartment on West Tenth Street, not knowing what was going to transpire in the coming days.

Tim reported back to Centre Street the next morning at 9:00 a.m. with a duffel bag full of clean underwear, socks, some basic toiletries and a few paperback books. *How did this happen to me?* he kept asking.

After a long boring day of questions by the attorneys and back-and-forth discussions with the judge in her chambers, the jurors were dismissed for the day to check into the Sheraton.

Tim got his key card, went up to his room and dumped his duffel bag on the bed. He opened the sliding glass doors to a small balcony overlooking the Hudson River. In the distance he could see the Statue of Liberty.

He was not interested in having dinner in the buffet dining room with the other jurors. Maybe he'd have a cheeseburger from room service if the court would pay for it. He dialed room service, and the voice at the other end said, "Yes, food is allowed, but no alcoholic beverages."

"Fine," Tim said. "Just a cheeseburger and a Coke."

"Pepsi all right?" was the response. "We don't carry Coke."

"Fine. Whatever," Tim answered as he hung up the phone. This was like being in prison.

Tim unpacked his duffel bag, put his clothes in the drawers

and then deposited the toilet kit in the bathroom. He had no idea how long he was going to be cooped up at the Sheraton, cut off from the outside world. The television had been removed from the room, and there were no newspapers—all because of a 270-pound raccoon.

The knock on the door came sooner than he had anticipated. A tall dyke with a short-cropped military haircut entered the room with a tray balanced on her shoulder.

"Where do you want it, Honey?" she asked.

"Oh, just on the desk over there," Tim said, a bit taken aback at her familiarity.

"Sure, kid," she said. "You got it. Jury duty?" she asked as she put the tray on the desk.

"Yeah," Tim answered. "I feel like I'm in prison."

"Well the Sheraton is a lot nicer than the real thing," she offered. "I know, Honey."

Tim didn't know what to say, but he got up and offered the woman a few dollars tip.

"We're not supposed to take tips from jurors," she said. "But then a girl has to eat." She smiled, pocketing the money. "Have a good night, Honey. You're really cute." She winked as she closed the door.

Well that was something, Tim thought. He pulled the chair up to the desk and opened the Pepsi. The fizzing bubbles were refreshing even though Tim would have preferred having a real drink. As he bit into the cheeseburger, there was a rattling sound on the sliding glass door off the balcony. Tim pulled the sheer curtain back to reveal a hunky, muscled guy on the terrace of his balcony. He slid the door half-open in amazement.

"Who are you?" Tim asked, even though he knew he had seen this person before. "And what are you doing outside my room?"

"I'm juror number eleven, and I'm in the room next door. I thought you might like some company, so I brought some wine," he said, referring to the bottle of chardonnay he was holding. "I just climbed over the balcony to come pay a visit. It's so boring here with no TV."

"Are you crazy?" Tim asked, astounded. "You could get killed."

"I'm actually Spiderman," he joked. "Are you going to ask me in?"

"Well, come in, I guess," Tim said, opening the sliding glass door all the way.

"Thanks. I saw you checking me out this afternoon in the jury box. I could tell," he teased mischievously.

"I was checking out the other jurors to see who they were," Tim admitted.

"And you knew. You got it right away." He smiled. "I'm Jackson Templeton. I know how pretentious that sounds. Just call me Jack."

"Hi. I'm Tim Halladay."

"Good to meet you."

"How did you get the wine?" Tim asked.

"I work on Wall Street. I know how to get things."

"I guess," Tim said.

"I found a way to get into the minibar without a key, the same way I found out how to open the adjoining door to our rooms. Open it up and we can have a suite here at the downtown Sheraton. And we can hang out together while we're deliberating over this 270-pound raccoon."

"That would be cool," Tim said. "But we're not supposed to talk about the case."

"What's to talk about? The guy murdered his battle-ax mother-in-law who'd been living with them for years. Then he claimed she was a raccoon. Do we really have to sit in court and hear all this bullshit while we're holed up here at the Sheraton every night?"

"So you've already made up your mind?" Tim asked as Jack poured him a glass of wine.

"Is the pope Catholic?" Jack winked, toasting Tim with the chardonnay.

"Well it does seem pretty obvious, but I think we have to look at all the evidence."

"How long will it take you to figure this situation out? Do we have to spend a week at the Sheraton to nail this guy?"

"Good point." Tim said, laughing. "First impressions are often pretty accurate. What do you do on Wall Street, when you're not on jury duty?" Tim asked curiously.

"I manage other people's money. I'm pretty good at it."

"I would think so."

"I know this guy is guilty, despite the wife's confession."

"How can you be so sure?" Tim asked.

"Well, I didn't connect it at first, but when the lawyers were going through all the questions, I remembered that the husband came into our office a few months ago to open a CD for two hundred thousand dollars. I handled the paperwork."

"So you knew this guy?"

"Not really. But at the time I thought it was kind of strange. I mean, he didn't look like the type of person who could just drop two hundred thousand dollars into a CD, coming in off the street. Something seemed wrong."

"So why didn't you excuse yourself when the lawyers asked if you had any knowledge of the case or the persons involved?"

"I wanted to see the dumb fuck go to jail. He's a real idiot," Jack said, pouring more wine. Not waiting for Tim to ask, he volunteered, "Married with three teenage girls. We live on Riverside Drive. Very traditional, upscale West Siders. You?"

"I live on Tenth Street in a small brownstone third-floor walk-up. I just lost my job in advertising before the holidays. Then this came up."

"Boyfriend?" Jack asked.

"Not really," Tim hedged. "But I've been seeing somebody, if you can call it that. Problem is, he lives in California."

"Sometimes the long-distance ones are the best."

"I don't know," Tim said uncertainly. "I guess we'll have to see."

"You're not going to have any trouble," Jack said, reaching out to pull Tim in front of him. Jack slowly undid the buttons on Tim's shirt, sliding his hand up Tim's chest under his T-shirt. "I saw you in the jury pool and wanted to meet you."

"But…" Tim started, and then Jack kissed him on the lips. The wineglasses fell on the carpet as the two embraced.

When Tim woke up they were both naked in bed. He looked at the alarm clock. It was after three in the morning, and they had to be back at the Court House at nine. Tim shook Jack's shoulder, gently waking him up.

"Hey guy…we have to pull this together."

"What? You worried about your civic duty?" Jack grinned with a sleepy smile, giving Tim a long, deep kiss.

"Well, I mean, we do have to show up."

"Don't worry, kid. We'll get there."

"Is this what they call jury tampering?" Tim smiled.

"No, guy. This is jury pampering," Jack said as he pulled Tim up against him in a firm, close embrace.

MOTORCYCLE MASH-UP

Guillermo Luna

Looking back, I should have immediately noticed him when I walked into the bar but my overwhelming need for liquor, any kind, focused my vision on the bartender and the alluring glow of the illuminated bar behind him. After I got my drink I sat near him but only because there was no one else in the bar. That's what I get for drinking *before* happy hour. What started, years ago, as a need to become more social has brought me to afternoons like this. His name was Duke and his large husky frame was partially hidden by not only the darkness of the room but also the fact that he was sitting down and his lower half was hidden behind the short part of an L-shaped bar.

He wasn't my type and it didn't help when he said he liked small, geeky guys with glasses. He had a shaved head, a ZZ Top beard, a pirate earring in his left ear and he wore a leather jacket, so I don't know why I agreed to go on a date with him. I glared at him when he called me "sweetie" instead of Rodrigo, but I have to admit I came to like that term of endearment simply because nobody had ever called me *that* before.

When he stood up I realized I had probably made a mistake. He was six foot four and at least 250 pounds. A looker? I don't know, but he did have a manly way about him. We talked outside the bar later that night and I did feel a twinge of something as I watched him PEEL out on his motorcycle. I continued to see him for a year. It was twelve months of drinks, cigarettes, fights, threats and getting banned from respectable establishments.

He was the jealous type. It stemmed from his insecurity at being such a big and frightful man and yet failing to be scary, almost disappointing really, in the one place that mattered most to men. The best example of his jealousy was when the two of us went out with my friend Andrew. Andrew was the one accused that night—just because he was there—and it ended with me pulling to a quick stop in a dark alley. The car was running and the lights were on when Andrew jumped out, followed by Duke. He chased Andrew around my Suzuki while stumbling in his big, Frankenstein, steel-toed motorcycle boots and threatening my friend with every drunken step.

That winter a motorcycle accident put a crimp in our routine.

Duke ended up in intensive care for two weeks and then was sent to a rehab facility out in Pomona for six months. I faithfully drove out to see him three or four times a week and witnessed many of the inappropriate comments that sprang from his foul mouth. Words and phrases that people normally suppress in public punctuated his rehab environment nonstop. The nurses seemed embarrassed even though they said they had heard it all before. The doctor said his brain was trying to find its way back but it was misfiring on its way there. When he was released he wanted to live with me. Since his father was elderly and his brother had a family of his own, it fell on me. Living together worked out for approximately ninety days. What wasn't working was his brain or at least not the way it had before. The salty language had stopped but he had brain damage on both sides and while he seemed perfectly fine to anyone who met him, if they talked to him for more than thirty minutes it became apparent that he wasn't fine. The clue was that he would repeat the same stories he had just told you minutes before.

My old dad once told me a story about how he learned to lay bricks. He didn't speak English at the time and the man who taught him didn't speak Spanish. "How did he teach you?" I asked. My old dad said, "Through patience and kindness." I don't possess those qualities.

When I couldn't handle Duke anymore—when it got to the point where I was slamming doors and throwing stuff—I contacted Duke's father and told him he *had* to take him. I couldn't take care of someone for the rest of my life whom I had only known for a year and a half, when I wasn't even married to the guy. It was an awkward and angry good-bye. He flew back to the Midwest and the memory of him and the good times we had together faded with the years until I was ordered into a 12-step program by the court.

I dreaded getting up, getting dressed and going to the nightly 12-step meetings once I found my way home (who wants to go out again once they've taken off their shoes?), so I started doing my wash three times a week. I would go from work *to* the Laundromat *to* my 12-step meeting. I had the cleanest clothes for the longest time. Luckily, I found a convenient Laundromat between the train station and my 12-step meeting place. The Laundromat was a dump. It was open twenty-four hours, without a guard on duty, so you can imagine its shape. I was standing out front waiting for my clothes to dry one evening when I saw him. He was sitting outside, far across a big parking lot, at one of those coffee places. I squinted my eyes to make sure it was him. It was.

How did he get back here? Did his father die? Maybe his brother who had a wife and kids didn't want a brain-damaged monster living with them? Whatever the reason, I stood watching him as he smoked a cigarette with an empty look on his face.

It was the same look he had *that* Christmas Eve. We had been at a place called The Tool, but after Duke got belligerent with the bartender we were immediately told to "*Get the fuck out.*" No warning, just "Get the fuck out." Duke didn't want to leave but when the bartender reached under the bar for a bat we both knew we wouldn't be closing this bar that night, so we stumbled across the street to this lesbian bar. It was a place called The Two of Hearts. The Two of Hearts was a neighborhood bar where they had poetry readings (female poets only), there was an active book club (uh, women authors), they mobilized politically (lady issues) and the smell of clove cigarettes permeated the place. Duke stormed toward The Two of Hearts front door ahead of me, at full throttle and pissed. He hit the door with the side of his balled-up fist with so much force that the door flew open, banged on the wall behind it and started to close again. That just made him angrier so he karate chopped the door as it advanced toward him with the side of his hand, and it flung back and banged against the wall again. He topped off his entrance with a bit of holiday cheer. I watched as he stood in the doorway and yelled, at the very top of his lungs, "MERRY FUCKING CHRISTMAS!!!!" Then he threw his head back like a drunk, unhinged Santa and started laughing. I followed Duke as he entered the bar and made his way through the crowd. The patrons treated him like royalty and this was patently evident when they scurried out of his way as he advanced toward them. They were a courteous group of lady lovers.

Behind the bar stood a tiny blonde with a flat top. Duke yelled his drink order at her as the whole jittery bar watched. She looked away, over her shoulder, but no one came to her aid. She didn't have a choice so she cleared her throat, but heaven help her, when she spoke it still came out high and pip-squeaky. She said it calmly, with her 105 pounds backing her up, "Sir, I cannot serve you a drink because you're drunk."

Duke blinked his eyes. It was as if he didn't understand what she was saying or he couldn't hear the high pitch of her voice. He looked at me with bloodshot eyes and a heaving chest. I did not respond so he turned away from me and lowered his whole upper body down onto the bar. He rested on his elbows so he could be face to face with her. When he opened his mouth he said only three words: "What the fuck?" The little bartender looked down before she turned to me and did something weasely and unfair: she pleaded with me, mutely, with her eyes. She wanted ME to help HER? Christ! I turned to Duke and pushed the arm that was closest to me off the bar. He glared at me. I said, "Would you stop bothering her? It's Christmas. Have a little decency."

I grabbed Duke by the arm of his leather jacket and pushed him toward a bar stool. He stumbled momentarily but regained his balance and responded by raising his arms in the air and saying very loudly, "HEY! HEY! HEY!" I ignored him, smiled at the bartender and said, "Can we get a couple of waters?"

I reached in Duke's pocket and pulled out his cigarettes. The corner of his top lip went up and exposed his teeth before he growled and said, "Give me a kiss." I looked up at him unsure of what I wanted to do so he pulled me toward him and I obliged. When I was released from his grip I lit a cigarette and put it in his mouth. Either the cigarette or the kiss placated him because he sat down and, with that act, all the fight oozed out of him. He sucked on the cigarette, exhaling the smoke at me. He looked exhausted. Under his breath I heard him mumble, "Merry Fucking Christmas," but it was missing all the bravado of the earlier one. He looked defeated and empty, so quietly, almost in a whisper, and just for him I began to sing, "Have Yourself a Merry Little Christmas"—but I did it in a very *manly* way. He listened to me as his smoke swirled around both of us. When I finished he put his cigarette out and took his large, beefy hand and gently brushed my hair away from my face. What must I have looked like? He sat in front of me sweaty and disheveled. He smelled of smoke. I raised my eyebrows and shrugged my shoulders at the whole situation. He continued to stare at me for the longest time in silence, then, rather lovingly, the big bear leaned forward and kissed me on the cheek.

He was scary and desirable at the same time. At bars, overeager guys would get shot down in front of me but, in the end, I was the one who was envied. He was what I wanted. Now, here he was again—fifty feet away. I was staring at him when he turned his head and looked in my direction. In that second I did what I had to do. I turned away. I turned away because I didn't want him to see me. I turned away because I wanted to forget him *and all of it*. But I turned away, mostly, because I couldn't care about him anymore. I had to save myself.

I raced back inside, frantically pulled my clothes out of the dryer, shoved the balled-up mess that's my life into a plastic laundry basket and fled out the back door.

ROMANCING OF THE HANDS

Raymond Luczak

The twinkle in his eyes shone in the picture above his online profile. More clicked pictures revealed a tall and fit man with a graying, trimmed beard standing astride his bicycle, smiling next to his children, and smooching a close woman friend. Hmm.

I had long been used to getting a lack of responses to my emails expressing interest, so I thought, *What the heck!*

I sent him an email with a link to my profile that indicated my deafness and my feelings about the bar scene (usually too dark to lip-read and too loud to hear anyone even with my residual hearing). Within minutes we were chatting online. We talked about our lives. He had raised three children and lived with two of them, who were nearing the end of their high school years. I had moved to Minneapolis the year before after having lived in New York for seventeen years. He was happily divorced. I had been in a fifteen-year relationship that ended amicably. He shared his Jungian perspective on life. I was intrigued, more so because he knew American Sign Language (ASL) and understood Deaf culture. It was an odd yet thrilling experience to find a hearing person teasing me about being Deaf; he was respectful with his inside knowledge.

Our first date a few days later in an Italian gourmet comfort café was awkward at best. We were both guarded, unsure about each other, even as our voiceless hands conveyed volumes about ourselves. Yet our weight of unspoken expectations seemed to color the Wednesday lunch atmosphere gray as if to complement the overcast clouds. We walked around my neighborhood and talked housing prices. He was in the market to buy a house after years of living in rented apartments and houses and taking care of his children. He was looking forward to having his own freedom back once his kids left the nest.

When we arrived at his car, he seemed to tower over me as he stroked my arm almost without warning, right there on Hennepin Avenue. He was two inches taller than I was, and I could not help but look up into his gray eyes. He gave me a smile so gentle and unexpected. I was quite taken aback by the tenderness in his hands as he touched me good-bye. Without dwelling on how awkwardly we had spent time together, I agreed to meet him again.

Two days later we biked around Cedar Lake. But first we went to a food co-op, bought ourselves lunch and loaded the picnic food up on his bike. As I watched him coast down the paved path winding around the lake, I was taken by the smooth beauty and shape of his shirtless back. He was justifiably proud of his chest. The more we wheeled, the more he began to flirt. He wriggled his ass at me, and made some sly comments about my body, as he would suddenly sail by. He knew that most hearing people wouldn't know what he said in ASL so it was like a secret language that no one knew.

The flirtations were intoxicating. Here I was, already forty years old, and it hit me that no one had ever tried to flirt with me so incessantly, and quite so openly. It seemed that dates consisted of two events (meeting and having sex), but here I was, in the limbo-land between meeting and conjugating. Sometimes we stopped and ate part of our picnic food before we moved on to the next lake. All told, we ended up going around three lakes and learning more about each other than we ever could have, had we stayed in restaurants each time we met. It was a joy to truly understand everything he said because he knew so well the language that I had been deprived of all my life, until I first came to Gallaudet University—the world's only liberal arts college for the Deaf—when I was eighteen.

Then we biked past Lake Calhoun, which often boasted an ongoing parade of lookers and onlookers usually wearing the ubiquitous white iPod headphones, on foot, rollerblades, and bikes.

Up the hill we climbed toward Lake Harriet. I saw how the unexpected sun cast a glint of glare in the rivulets of sweat winding down his back. Then down and around the lake we wove under the hanging trees until we stopped at the bandstand.

No one sat on the stage so we did, and ate ice cream, and melded our hands. I told him more than I'd told most people, and he told me more than I'd expected to hear. Family dynamics in our pasts had shaped us differently for different reasons, but I understood his frustrations. I was surprised when he opened my legs on the edge of the stage and pulled me closer to him for a kiss.

I was surprised by his need, and I still hadn't finished my bowl of ice cream!

I was used to being discreet with my desire for another in public, especially now that I was no longer living in the more gay-friendly Manhattan. I was floored by his flattery.

By the time we parted, six hours had passed. I felt giddy when I saw him leave with his bike hitched to the back of his car. What had I missed from all those years when I was single and dating? A giggly light-headedness that I didn't think was quite possible. I was forty years old, for god's sake!

A few days later he showed up at my apartment for dinner. We didn't say a word as he crossed the threshold into my arms. We embraced for a few minutes, and in that fleeting moment I closed my eyes and inhaled the scent of his cologne-free neck. I felt his heart throb slightly against my chin and the smooth inclines of his back. I thought of nothing but the sweet musk of his smell wafting into the deep seat of my brain and down into my groin.

As much as I didn't want to, I finally broke away. The logistics of cooking my first meal for him had encroached on my mind. I hadn't yet heated up the electric stove top or taken out the pair of tuna steaks upon which I would toss a few drops of toasted sesame oil and some beef broth for a pan sauce, adding some pimentos and capers. Simple, perhaps, but incredibly effective as a quick dinner.

He said, "That was a really good hug. You didn't hold back anything. Let's do it again."

We hugged, this time for a longer time. I've hugged all my boyfriends and partners, but never as long as I did with him while standing and so we felt still as time itself. I felt bathed in that warm light emanating from the kitchen table. The world was full of shadow but there he stood like a beacon in my arms. I looked up at him, and we kissed. Simply and lightly.

We smiled quietly at each other. There was absolutely no pressure to do more than leave a lingering mark on each other's lips.

He kicked off his sandals and walked barefoot across the carpet to my leather love seat.

I brought out a small bowl containing kalamata olives heated in two quick turns in my microwave oven and an empty ramekin for the pits. I placed them on the coffee table in front of my love seat.

He sat down on one end as I placed a warm olive into his mouth. His lips pursed around my fingertips as he looked up into my eyes. His eyes widened at the burst of unexpectedly strong olive flavors on his tongue, and then he grinned. I held the ramekin in front of him where he let the pit drop from his mouth. He beckoned for another olive from me and as he took it with his teeth, his tongue suddenly darted out to lick my fingertips. His eyes never strayed from mine as his tender taste buds curled around the pistils of my hands opening up like a flower.

I leaned down and kissed him.

He lathered my tongue with olives grown in Spain and imported to a local shop near my home, the kind of place that had made such miracles of being all over the world at once and yet not far beyond the confines of my kitchen possible. His tongue was a foreign country with unfamiliar scents, quite different from the waft of his neck earlier.

He broke the kiss, spit out the pit and brought a fresh olive up to my lips. This I took with my teeth, and I expertly bit its purple flesh off the stone pit. I let it fall out of my mouth into the ramekin, and then our tongues danced a tango as our arms melded around each other's bodies on the sofa. Once the olive was finally consumed, I rested lightly atop his chest and closed my eyes. I imagined that I was outside somewhere under an olive tree—even though I'd yet to see one in my life. His hands slid slowly around the contours of my back and I sensed his sighing.

The reality of how cramped we were on the love seat finally broke our spell.

I guided myself off him and realized that I'd forgotten to do one other thing. I plugged in the white Christmas lights that I'd hung all around my four windows. He took off his shirt without any ado and lay there, his face softly lit and his eyes almost as bright. I fed him another olive, and while we signed to each other, we took turns feeding each other the ever-cooling olives still seeped in their juices.

Sips from our glasses of ice-laden water refreshed our mood as we chatted between bites of a chopped green pepper, which I had wanted to use up—it wouldn't belong in the salad I was to make. The sudden crunchiness of cool pepper was a contrast to the warm tanginess of olive. As I sat there admiring his lazy chest, I found his hand holding my left as I signed with my right. Even though ASL usually requires both hands for unencumbered communication, context often enables the other person to fill in mentally the other half of the two-hand signs used when one hand is occupied with something else: he understood me perfectly.

A dream had come true, hadn't it? A handsome hearing man could understand me perfectly without the need for me to use my voice, and he was so fluent in ASL that I didn't need to use both hands to be understood! There weren't many of those out there.

As I chopped up shallots and whirred a blend of olive oil and balsamic vinegar in a mini food processor to create the salad dressing in the kitchen, he took my salad spinner and spun its wet greens so much that each leaf bounced to the bottom of the colander with springiness. I showed him where he could mix the greens and other ingredients before he poured the dressing.

He knew how much I couldn't get enough of his naked chest

so he took every opportunity to rub his pectorals across my back or display himself, leaning against the cupboard above the sink, watching me sear the sashimi-quality tuna steaks quickly into a pastel brown with quite pink centers. His half-naked body distracted me but I managed to not scorch the pan sauce and poured it over both of our plates when he sat down at the table. I felt secretly proud of not having made a cooking mistake thus far and having been able to put together a decent meal—even on a first dinner date. As we ate, we held hands across the narrow table: a single lamp shone on our food and lent a soft glow to both our faces.

No one asked to take an instant photograph of us.

No one offered us roses for sale.

No one sang an Italian aria before our table.

All that silence was quite all right with us.

As we ate, we signed and smiled and stared into each other's eyes. The world—however small it had been in our hands that moment—was fleetingly ours that night, that gem-like transcendence of memory forever mine. That night our hands spoke louder than words.

THE GREAT MASTURBATOR

Daniel M. Jaffe

Before I met The Great Masturbator at the circus, I used to wonder if I'd ever know romance. In this age of quickie Internet hookups, how did you find a man for whom "body contact" was more than a contact sport? For whom affection was not an STD? I longed to stare into another man's eyes and watch his essence overlap my reflection for hours. To slip my tongue between his lips, to taste him, his saliva mixing with mine, each of us swallowing us both together. To feel that initial heart-skip percolation burble with the potential to boil into love after a lengthy simmer. Where was my fantasy man? Had love-seekers been killed off by climate change?

I'll never forget the Saturday night we met six months ago, The Great Masturbator and I. I'd finished yet another eight-hour day ringing up underwear sales at Old Navy. Haggard mothers swatting whiney children in line. Oh-so-clever, shaved-head gangbanger shoplifters paying for one marked-down T-shirt while thinking I wouldn't notice the other one stuffed down their pants—I admire big baskets as much as anyone but... To make the day extra special, my manager had threatened to fire me after I returned fifteen minutes late from lunch. True, I'd been engrossed in stories about the traveling Folsom Circus, but who could resist reading about THE CIRCUS OF THE LOST, as the Southern California tabloids dubbed it?

Supposedly, wherever the traveling Folsom Circus performed, some local man disappeared. Headline after headline told the tale: I LOST MY PARTNER TO THE FOLSOM CIRCUS! (A superior court judge in Ventura left the county courthouse on his Harley one evening, drove to the circus, but never returned to his chambers or home. His Harley went missing, too.) GONE WITH THE TRAVELING CIRCUS WIND! (In San Diego one breezy day, a churro vendor took his little girls to the Folsom Circus and left them watching a magic show while he went off to see "some other act." He never picked his daughters up, nor was he seen anywhere again.) THE GREATEST VANISHING ACT ON EARTH! (In Palm Springs, police investigated the disappearance of an elderly couple—wrinkly owners of a clothing-optional, men-only resort—last seen hobbling into the Big Top. No trace even of their walkers with yellow half–tennis balls stuck on the aluminum feet.)

Some cities called in the FBI to pitchfork through turd-filled hay piles in the elephant stalls, to claw through the lions' food fridge and then DNA test mounds of raw meat. Not a flake of human skin, not a broken human hair follicle: nada.

I'd long been a fan of "The Twilight Zone" and "X-Files." Could any of this tabloid stuff really have happened? Fun to think so, but it was probably all made up. Even if those folks had actually gone missing, that was just coincidence. Most likely, the circus promoters themselves had started the rumors about missing people. Scary sells—a Hollywood maxim.

Not that the circus had to rely on phony hype, as far as I was concerned. Any circus with an act called The Great Masturbator was sure to be a sellout, given the number of perverts here in California. Of which I was surely one. I was intrigued by the tabloids' descriptions of his "unusual self-pleasuring techniques" and "one-of-a-kind moving body art you've got to see to believe."

My interest wasn't piqued just because of the whole sexual aspect—heavens no! Not at all. I wasn't that shallow, was I? No, I told myself, I was fascinated by the whole marketing approach. After all, in college I'd been a marketing major, which was why I'd expected to become the next hotshot somebody in a "Mad Men" agency. "The world is your oyster," said the oh-so-original Dean at graduation three years ago. Unfortunately, he failed to anticipate that the oyster I'd happen to crawl into would wash up on shore and rot in its own stink under the morning sun. I was becoming nobody fast.

Not that anyone really noticed or cared. My parents have had nothing to do with me for years: "Homosexual abominations are doomed to a life of loneliness and we refuse to witness such a tragedy befall our very own son." (Was it the befalling of the tragedy they minded, or the watching of it?)

My charming roommate noticed me only when the landlady pounded on the door for the rent. "Hey, Dude," he'd say to me between smoke-sucking joint inhalations, "could you front my half again this month?"

And it's not as though I had any romantic attachments, although I was usually able to find sex on those nights I felt so overwhelmed with desire I could think of nothing else. Those nights, I'd pound away at the keyboard answering any online ad I could find for a well-endowed muscle top. I needed to take a man deep inside, and wished I were an octopus—I'd need at least eight arms to clasp him close enough to satisfy myself. On the drive home after the hookup, I'd inevitably feel an emptiness no man was big enough to fill.

So, that Saturday night six months ago, exhausted from a lousy day at work and full of curiosity prompted by the tabloids, I went straight to the circus instead of returning home. I bought my requisite pink cotton candy (ever since I was a child, no carnival or fair was complete without pink cotton candy), then I poked into a tent to see the obligatory bearded lady in leopard-print cave-woman garb. Big deal, a transgendered person in fake fur.

Another tent housed Siamese twins supposedly joined at a hip that just happened to be covered by a shared, blousy, green-sequined tunic. I recognized the brothers who ran our local Thai restaurant, one in charge of the front of the house, the other who cooked in back.

So far, this circus was lame.

I had to show ID to enter the big tent, which smelled like sweat and elephant shit (not that I could really distinguish elephant shit from lion's or any other animal's). I practically buried my nose in the cotton candy while stumbling up the bleachers to an empty seat in the very last row, far from the various animals dancing on hind legs down front. Prancing ponies in spangled harnesses; dogs climbing on each other's backs; a blond guy in a white leotard doing the obligatory shove-your-head-in-the-lion's mouth. I hadn't come here for schlock; from the looks of the yawning, fidgety crowd, neither had anyone else.

The old guy seated next to me, in a red flannel shirt and suspenders, offered me popcorn from a paper bag. I declined. "Can I taste your cotton candy?" he asked. What could I say? Rather than let him take a bite, I pulled off a fluffy wad and handed it over. "Yum," he said. "Good as I remember from childhood." Whatever.

Applauding as lion and tamer exited, the emcee in red tails and black boots took his place under the central spotlight. "And now, ladies and gentlemen, the *pièce de résistance*." Finally. "The act you've all been waiting for. The pride and joy of the traveling Folsom Circus." This better be good. "The one! The only! The unforgettable—Salvador, The Great Masturbator!" The emcee extended his white-gloved hand up toward the tent's inner peak.

We all tilted our heads back and looked up to see the underside of a red-velvet throne with a baroque gold frame. Now, that was something. The throne descended on ropes while bare feet and calves dangled in front of it. Broad, high-arched feet. Thickly muscled calves. My breath quickened. The throne reached ground level, and my heartbeat sped up. Finally, the real deal, something worth the price of admission: an enormous muscle man in a simple Tarzan loincloth. His thighs were huge and perfectly shaped. His six-pack rippled, and his chest muscles—each one stretched like the expanse of the Russian Steppes. Sculpted arms, square jaw, wavy black hair brushed back on the sides to rest on his shoulders. A hero out of the Hercules movies I'd gorged on during adolescence.

The Great Masturbator's green eyes glistened under the spotlight. How beautiful he was. How totally beautiful. He looked slowly around the crowd, first scanning the semicircle of lower bleachers, then the middle ones and then the upper ones where I sat in shadow. I could have sworn that his eyes lingered on mine. Mine? No! Ridiculous! Wishful thinking, that's all. Mine? No. Maybe? I sort of felt his gaze reach to my lips and gently brush them. Was that possible? No way. Yes. Definitely. I swallowed hard as I felt his stare part my lips, even slide into my mouth and down my throat.

When he moved his eyes away from mine to complete a scan

of the upper bleachers, I felt something rip from me, from deep inside, as though a predator had torn out an organ through my throat. The cotton candy slipped from my sweating hands, dropped onto my lap.

"Careful," whispered the old guy in suspenders beside me. "Don't want to get all sticky pants."

I shook my head in numb agreement.

"Ladies and gentlemen," asked the emcee, "are you ready?"

"Yes," murmured some in the crowd. "Yes! Yes!" from men and women both.

Seated in his baroque red-velvet throne, The Great Masturbator splayed the fingers of his right hand, waved it like a magic wand over his loincloth-covered crotch.

"Do you want to see it?" asked the MC.

"You betcha!"—from a short-haired, redheaded woman in the front row.

"Show us already!"—from a heavyset blonde woman on the far left.

"Whip it out!"—from a middle-aged bald man two rows below me.

"If you want it," cried the emcee, "then you gotta beg for it!"

"C'mon!" called out the short-haired redhead in the front row, "Let's see!"

"We paid the price of admission!" cried the heavyset blonde woman, "So give."

From the corner of my eye, I could see the old man in suspenders beside me shift the bag of popcorn over his crotch, then slip his hand beneath it.

"If you really want it," the emcee ordered the redheaded woman in the front row, "then get on your knees and prove it!"

Laughing, she did so. She even flapped her hands in abandoned frenzy.

"That a girl!" cried the emcee. "That's what we need! Give the lady a hand, ladies and gentlemen. Thanks to her, you will all be granted witness!"

The spotlight that had been encircling the entire throne now telescoped onto The Great Masturbator's loincloth. He reached his right hand beneath it, massaged without revealing.

Sudden silence in the tent. Complete silence.

He withdrew his right hand, slipped an index finger between his lips, sucked it down to the knuckle, in and out, again and again. The spotlight telescoped onto his finger. He held that wet finger aloft as if testing how the wind blew, lifted his left arm and flexed, traced the right finger along the inside of the bulging left bicep, leaving a snail-track of saliva. The bicep came to life. I don't mean that it simply pulsed or danced the way biceps do when flexed—it did that, but much more: on the skin's surface a swirl of colors emerged, a twirling kaleidoscope of grays and blacks and pinks that gradually...took the shape...of a man. A chubby man in profile. On a motorcycle. Naked, but for a helmet.

The spotlight widened. Holding his left arm aloft, The Great Masturbator returned his right hand beneath the loincloth. The chubby man on the bicep kick-started his motorcycle—we could even hear the engine roar, see exhaust drift out the back and disappear into The Great Masturbator's hairy armpit. The chubby motorcyclist sat and—oh my god—masturbated. His masturbation rhythm kept pace with that of The Great Masturbator beneath his loincloth until The Great Masturbator stopped. The roar of the motorcycle engine diminished to a whir, the chubby rider heaved and swallowed, and then...slowly dissolved into a swirl of colors, disappearing back into The Great Masturbator's raised bicep.

Everyone remained stock-still. What had we just witnessed?

What *was* this? Had some movie camera been projecting images onto that bicep? I looked up at the light beaming from the tent ceiling lamps—no, no colors, just a (an ordinary?) yellow beam.

The Great Masturbator smiled a wry grin, again scanned the crowd as he'd done at his act's beginning, and once again, when his eyes reached mine, I felt him linger, lock onto them. This time, my breathing stopped as he did so. Had he reached out and pressed his hand over my nose and mouth, he couldn't have stopped my breathing more completely. I grew dazed, and the outline of his being grew fuzzy. When he looked away, I felt as if a pressed pillow had been lifted from my face. I let out a rush of withheld air, inhaled deeply.

The Great Masturbator switched hands now, raised his right bicep, slipped a left finger into mouth, traced saliva along the flexing bicep, then reached his left hand beneath loincloth to masturbate. Again a swirl of colors on his bicep, this time of a mustachioed man, naked and thin, a churro upheld in each hand. As The Great Masturbator continued massaging himself beneath the loincloth, the churro holder slipped one churro into his mouth and fellated it, then bent over, slipped the second churro into his backside and pumped. In and out, in and out with growing frenzy until, as before, The Great Masturbator ceased his own masturbation. Churro Man froze still, dissolved into swirls of color and disappeared on the bicep.

The crowd began to applaud. I joined in, hesitantly—was this titillating or vulgar? Both? I thought of those tabloid reports of the missing judge on his Harley and the missing dad with his two churros. More than coincidence, clearly, but what did it all mean? Had The Great Masturbator, after reading the tabloid reports, somehow painted movable disappearing tattoos on his biceps? Or had the tabloid reporters simply seen the act I'd just witnessed and made up the stories so as to scandalize?

As if reading my thoughts, The Great Masturbator stared at me with an almost mocking smile. Woozy, I wobbled in place. He looked away.

He stood now, and his loincloth bulged.

"Take it off!" cried the heavyset blonde woman on the far left.

"You just gotta show us!" yelled the redhead still on her knees down front.

"Yeah," yelled the middle-aged man two rows below as he ran palm along his now heavily sweating bald head, "let's see what you're packin'!"

The Great Masturbator lifted his left leg to rest one foot on the red-velvet throne seat. A spotlight shone on thigh muscle. He slipped his right finger into his mouth and this time traced saliva along his thigh. Hand under loincloth, massage.

The now routine swirl of colors on his left leg transformed into two wrinkly men lying head-to-foot atop two walkers set apart like sawhorses. Yellow half–tennis balls spun and spun on the walkers' aluminum feet. Slowly, the men shifted from side-by-side to a clear 69 position, one on his back, the other on hands and knees above. Each fellated the other and this time, groans emanated from The Great Masturbator's body, moans and slurps and gurgles. As The Great Masturbator sped up his masturbation, the two old men's heads bobbed faster and faster. The Great Masturbator slowed his rhythm, and the two old men's head movements slowed as well. The Great Masturbator stopped completely and, predictably, the old men swirled back into colors, faded into flesh. He brought his leg down, stood straight, bowed.

The old man in suspenders beside me leapt to his feet and applauded. His popcorn spilled (and flew?) everywhere. The rest of the crowd gave a standing ovation, too. As did I, my cotton candy slipping from my lap to the bleacher floor. I'd never seen anything like this before. Had never imagined such a phenomenon. This was really happening; no movie projectors, no gimmicks. Or if there were, they were impossible to detect. It was either the best magic trick ever or the most amazing sex show on earth. Just amazing. Unbelievable. Mesmerizing. "Encore!" I blurted. "Encore!"

The crowd took up my chant, matching word to applause so that we were now clapping in rhythmic unison. "Encore! Encore! Encore!"

The Great Masturbator looked at the MC and nodded.

"He's consented, ladies and gentlemen!" the emcee declared into the microphone. "The Great Masturbator has consented to one more demonstration of his unique prestidigitation. Please take your seats."

We quickly obliged.

I expected him to look at me, The Great Masturbator. I just felt that he would, that somehow I had come to serve as his...I don't know...his erotic inspiration, his carnal muse. But he didn't look at me this time, and I felt a profound disappointment.

Again the finger-in-mouth ritual. This time a trace along the broad expanse of his right pectoral. Which shape would those color swirls take on next, an orgy? How many men could fit on that enormous half-chest? How would they undulate and in what sort of frenzy?

The colors gelled into the image of a man's upper body and head, like a sculptor's upper torso bust. This time, the face that appeared was The Great Masturbator's own. A replica of his own square-jawed face, muscled neck and shoulders and arms. Initially, the replica was facing front, but as The Great Masturbator massaged himself beneath loincloth, the replica face turned in profile to look across at the unoccupied left pectoral. The replica's muscled arms lifted, stretched out hands toward the blank left breast, reaching, straining toward the very sternum, unable to cross its muscle-knot ridges.

"He's lonely!" exclaimed the heavy blonde woman at the far left. "That's what it means! Poor man, he's lonely."

The old man in suspenders beside me sighed and nodded. "Indeed," he muttered, "aren't we all?"

"Take me!" yelled the redheaded woman, her arms out in pleading. "Place me on your chest! I'll love you forever!"

The replica face on the half-chest turned full front again. This time, it stared out at me, that replica face with heavy lids, half-hooded eyes of longing. Longing for me? What was I seeing? What was I imagining?

The replica's lips, thick now and pouting, opened as if to speak. The Great Masturbator ceased his stroking, and the replica face faded away into his chest.

The Great Masturbator then slipped the finger into his mouth, all the while locking his eyes onto mine. He traced the wet finger along his left pectoral, above his heart. No swirl of colors. Nothing. Blank skin.

For the first time, he withdrew his erection from beneath the loincloth and we all spontaneously gasped at the enormity we'd long suspected, the thickness, the smoothness, the perfection of male shape. Women in the audience wept, men shifted in their seats, likely mortified at the contrast between his ideal and their real. The old man beside me snapped his suspenders sharply against his chest, twice, as if testing that he was really awake.

I felt dizzy.

The Great Masturbator slid his left index finger into his mouth once more, withdrew it wet, but now extended his left palm out, straight to me as if in invitation to dance. A caress crossed my lips, tickled my tongue and palate, filled my throat, descended deep into my core to my groin, cupped my genitals from within, fondled them, squeezed almost to pain, kept me teetering on the threshold, tugging and pulling harder and slowly yanking my maleness through me until I felt The Great Masturbator's hand pull them up out my throat and my mouth, turning me inside out, revealing the side of me no one's ever witnessed, the inside that not even I had seen.

At the same moment, he pursed his lips as if to whistle, but did not blow out. Instead, he inhaled and I felt the draw. My body lifted. He was sucking me toward him! To his wind tunnel, to his whirlpool vortex, to the very eye of the tornado that was he. I felt myself suspended upside down in midair. I clutched at my seat bottom, but couldn't grasp it, succeeded only in snatching my dropped pink cotton candy. I flew down over the bleachers, over the sobbing and sweating middle-aged bald man, over the entire crowd; I sailed, completely inside out, down toward The Great Masturbator until I crashed smack against him, flew directly into the heat of his chest, permeated his skin, swam deep into his muscle, reached out my legs, entwined and hooked them around his thick nipple from the underside. My flight stopped. I came to rest. The pink cotton candy hung, suspended inches from my face.

What had just happened?

I looked out at the crowd, but not from my former perspective of the last and highest bleacher seat. No, I was not looking from behind at all; now I saw not backs and tops of heads as before, but faces. Blank faces. Faces of expectation. Faces in wait. Not faces that had just watched a man's solo flight over a crowd, but faces waiting to see something amazing.

Had they not seen me? Had they not witnessed my immersion into him? I looked to the old man in suspenders on the last row of the bleachers. He casually crossed his skinny legs, not seeming to notice that I was in any way missing. Or that I'd even been sitting there in the first place.

Had everything actually happened or had I been imagining? Had I fainted at some point? Was this reality or fantasy? Was I dreaming, hallucinating while in a semi-awake stupor? Or was I even lying in a coma somewhere, living exclusively within my own mind?

No. This was real. It had happened. Every bit of it. Whether others in the audience had witnessed or not, this had happened. I knew because I was there. It had happened to me.

The Great Masturbator's finger, wet and glistening, moved toward his chest, toward me. The finger traced along my forehead, my brows, my lips.

I turned my face to the side, saw that his right pectoral face replica had now reappeared and was staring at me, smiling, with arms outstretched. I lifted my own arms, reached out toward him, and our fingers nearly met at the muscle-knot ridge of his sternum. Nearly. But our fingers couldn't quite reach. Couldn't quite touch. I strained, undulated and thrashed within his muscle, his flesh, inside him, against him, all as the beating of his heart quickened and pounded and deafened me. I could smell him, the sweat dripping down his chest over me, his sweat of passion, possession. Still, our fingertips couldn't touch. Abruptly, The Great Masturbator gave a quick bow to the crowd and left the tent for his dressing room.

Was he as frustrated as I?

As he left the tent and strode to his trailer, I quickly receded, faded from his surface into a dark place within him, a quiet spot encompassed by the pulsations of blood-flow through muscle. No sound save those pulsations, a remarkably sustaining sound even as it calmed. I felt strangely at peace and, for the first time in my life, no longer alone.

Me. He'd chosen me. Of everyone under the big top that night, he'd selected me. Yet...why no climax? Had he been tired, perhaps, from the prior performance? Or might he have delayed the completion of our unity out of some romantic notion? I was willing to wait in darkness.

And I did, immobile except for my ability to nibble the forever regenerating pink cotton candy suspended beside my face. I passed time wondering exactly what had happened, in wonderment at all that had happened.

During his performance the next evening, he drew only me to life, none of the others. Not the chubby motorcyclist, not Churro Man, not the old 69-ers. I felt so proud. I seemed to spend hours on his chest, staring across into his replica eyes, stretching out my arms, reaching to embrace that replica while the real Great Masturbator stroked. Would he stroke to climax this time? And when he did, would our fingers magically clasp on his chest and interlock forever? Would our lips touch?

But as he'd done the previous night, he stopped abruptly, bowed and left.

This became our routine. Evening after evening, he'd bring me to life, energizing me more alive than I'd ever been when out of his body and alone. I experienced increasing anguish at seeing my other half just within reach yet never quite within my grasp.

Night after night.

In all these months, he's never stroked to climax, whether unable or choosing not to, I can't know because I have no way to ask. Having taken possession of me, he's silenced me.

I console myself with the thought that he knows what's best, that his repeated coitus interruptus has actually been for my benefit, for ours: perhaps fulfillment of our desire, even once, would cause me to lose myself and disappear within him forever?

That could be it. And that would explain why, over time, he's taken to summoning me with decreasing frequency—he must be trying to avoid the temptation of achieving a devastating fulfillment that's too overwhelming to resist. Yes, he wants to keep me with him always. That's why he never reaches climax with me, that's why he summons me forth less and less often. Because he treasures me. Yes, that must be it. He cherishes me so much that he can't bear to achieve fulfillment with me and risk my disappearance.

That's what I tell myself every evening as our circus travels from town to town. I now spend the vast majority of my time alone within his chest, comforting my loneliness with my reasoning and the inexhaustible supply of pink cotton candy.

Night after night, I sense The Great Masturbator staring out into the crowd, seeking someone new to imbed in his neck or shoulder or foot. One day he'll run out of blank skin for others to inhabit, and he'll have to settle for those of us already accumulated over the years, especially me. I'm his favorite, after all; I can just tell.

Maybe, at some point, he will even climax once with each of the others in order to cause them to explode and fade away forever. Then he'll spend the rest of his life with only me, just me, making love night after night with me. Never quite completing our desire, but resting happy in the knowledge that by holding back, we're sustaining our love in perpetuity.

I live in hope.

READER, I MARRIED HIM

Michael Thomas Ford

"Come on," Dorrie said, taking Adam by the hand and pulling him toward the back deck. "There's a guy I want to introduce you to."

Adam groaned. "Not again," he said. "The last time you played matchmaker you set me up with a guy who voted for Reagan."

"How was I supposed to know he was a Republican?" said Dorrie. "He was in a women's studies class. Anyway, Jay is different. You're going to love him."

Adam decided not to argue. He'd been friends with Dorrie long enough to know that it wouldn't matter anyway. Once she got an idea in her head the only thing you could do was go along with her or stay out of the way and hope you weren't dragged into whatever crazy idea she was following to its inevitably disastrous conclusion.

I'll just meet the guy, talk to him for a few minutes, then make an excuse to leave, he thought. *I'll say I have a pile of papers to grade.*

The deck was crowded with smokers. Dorrie, fearing the wrath of both her landlord and her vegan roommate, forbade smoking in the house. As a result, quite a number of the party guests were outside lighting up. The air was rich with the scent of pot, and the easy laughter of the deeply stoned echoed through the yard.

Dorrie approached a guy who was leaning against the railing that ran around the porch. Tall and dark haired, with a beard and hair that both wanted cutting, he wore jeans and a faded black T-shirt with the Cheap Trick logo on it. He was alone, but he didn't seem at all self-conscious or concerned about it. When he saw Dorrie a lopsided smile crossed his face, as if he'd been expecting her.

"Adam," Dorrie said. "This is Jay. Jay, this is Adam. Go."

She turned and walked away, leaving them alone. Adam said, "And there goes Hurricane Dorrie, leaving chaos in her wake."

Jay laughed. "I take it you two have been friends for a long time."

"About five years," said Adam. "We met as undergrads. Then we both ended up here for grad school. Different departments, of course."

"You're in the MFA program, right?" Jay said.

Adam nodded. "Working on the Great American Novel," he joked. "What about you?"

"Poli-sci," Jay answered. "But I'm only doing it because accumulating a mountain of student loan debt I have no intention of paying back is easier than figuring out what I want to be when I grow up." He took a hit from the joint in his hand, exhaled, and added, "Besides, I like the idea of using government money to buy pot. It's my personal 'fuck you' to Nancy Reagan."

He held out the joint and Adam took it. "Just say yes," said Adam, mocking the first lady's simplistic antidrug message.

"I like your accent," Jay said as Adam held the smoke in for as long as he could. "It's sexy."

"Sexy?" Adam said, choking as he laughed at Jay's comment. "It's been called a lot of things, but never sexy."

"Well, it is," said Jay. "Where are you from?"

"West Virginia," Adam answered. "And before you ask, no, my parents aren't brother and sister."

"I wasn't going to ask that," Jay told him, taking the joint back. "Do I look like I would say something so stupid?"

"Sorry," said Adam, embarrassed. "I didn't mean anything by it. I'm just used to people—"

"I was going to guess cousins," Jay said, interrupting him and grinning.

Adam laughed. "You dick," he said.

Over the course of the next half hour Adam learned that Jay was twenty-one, from a small town in upstate New York, had a sister who was born on the same date (October 9) but was seven years younger, thought U2 were overrated, didn't own a television, loved Thai food but was ambivalent about Mexican, and lived by himself in the attic apartment of an elderly lesbian couple who owned a huge Victorian house and rented out the six bedrooms they didn't use to grad students. Although they normally didn't rent to men, they'd made an exception for Jay because when he'd come by to ask about the apartment their ancient pugs, Alice and Gertrude, had taken a liking to him.

"I'm the only thing in the house with a penis," Jay said regarding his living situation. "They just pretend I'm a woman. They call me Bertha Rochester."

Adam snorted. "That's brilliant."

Jay cocked his head. "It is?" he said.

"Totally," said Adam. "You're the madwoman in the attic. You know, from *Jane Eyre*. Bertha Rochester."

"I just assumed they made it up," Jay replied. "I didn't know she was a real person."

"Well, she isn't *real*," said Adam. "She's a character in a book. She was Rochester's first wife, who went crazy and was basically locked in the attic with a nurse to look after her. She ended up burning down the house."

Jay laughed. "Now that I know that, it's funny," he said. "All this time I was annoyed that they thought I would be a Bertha."

"You've really never read *Jane Eyre*?" Adam asked.

Jay shook his head. "I'm more of a Douglas Adams, Frank Herbert, Stephen King kind of guy," he said. "Does that disqualify me?"

"From what?" Adam asked.

"From going home with you," said Jay. "I'd ask you back to my place, but the ladies wouldn't be too thrilled about sweaty man-sex going on over their heads. And I can get a little loud."

Adam didn't know what to say. He wasn't accustomed to such directness. Also, it had been quite some time since he'd either made or been made such an offer. He found himself tongue-tied.

"It's okay if you're not into me," Jay said. "It wouldn't be the first time a guy turned me down. But it never hurts to ask."

"No," said Adam. "It's not that. Not at all. You just caught me off guard."

Jay reached out and grabbed Adam's belt, pulling him in. He kissed Adam gently, then more intensely as Adam opened his mouth. Adam felt himself start to get hard. Jay's hand slid down and cupped him.

"So you *are* into me," he said.

They didn't even say good-bye to Dorrie. Leaving the party, they walked the four blocks to the small house Adam shared with another student from the English department, a girl named Valerie who was so quiet and shy that she rarely left her bedroom except to attend class.

"It's like living with a cat," Adam said as he unlocked the door.

They headed straight for the bedroom, where Adam shut the door before turning on the stereo and slipping a CD in.

"The Cure?" Jay said as he pulled his T-shirt over his head, exposing a torso thickly covered in hair.

"You like them?" asked Adam, sitting on the edge of the bed and removing his shoes.

"If they put you in the mood, I do," Jay said, kneeling behind him and beginning to unbutton Adam's shirt.

Adam leaned into Jay and let him undress him. Jay's hands moved over Adam's chest, his fingers stroking the hair there and teasing Adam's nipples. Then Jay's mouth was on his neck, biting gently. Jay's beard tickled. Adam was instantly hard.

Adam lay back on the bed and Jay slid on top of him. Fingers sought out buttons and zippers, and jeans were tossed to the floor. Adam's boxers followed. He was aroused by the fact that Jay wore nothing beneath his jeans, and that he didn't shave.

The night unfolded in slow motion, and Adam experienced it as he might a movie, a long, continuous shot of hands and mouths exploring, of legs and arms entwined, of sweat-slicked skin and damp armpits and tongues easing open musky passages and finally the sweet stickiness and breathlessness of release. Afterward they sprawled in a tangle of sheets, Jay's head resting on Adam's belly as he played with Adam's cock. The CD was on its second time through, and Robert Smith was singing about strange angels dancing in the deepest oceans.

"I love that you're uncut," Jay said, his fingers sliding

Adam's foreskin over the head of his dick and then pulling it back again.

"A lot of guys are freaked out by it," said Adam.

Jay traced the line of fur from Adam's crotch to his navel, swirling the cum-drenched hair into tiny peaks. "I think it's beautiful," he said.

Adam didn't know how to respond. Calling a cock beautiful seemed somehow inappropriate, but he loved that Jay had said it. "I should get a towel," he said, and started to get up.

"Stay there," Jay ordered. He leaned over and picked up his T-shirt, then used it to wipe Adam clean. "Now whenever I wear this I'll think of the night we met," he said.

"Such a romantic," said Adam, running his fingers through Jay's hair and looking into his eyes, which he saw now were a rich brown color, the black pupils like things caught and held forever in amber.

Jay tossed the shirt on the floor and stretched out beside Adam. Adam looked at their legs, noting the difference between Jay's tanned skin and dark hair and his own pale skin and red hair. He wondered if Jay wanted to spend the night. He was going to ask, then stopped and asked himself if he wanted Jay to stay. He was a little surprised to find that he did. And because he wanted it, he was now afraid to ask.

"Why do you think it's so easy for gay men to end up in bed together after they've just met?" Jay asked.

Adam, thankful for the distraction of the question, thought for a moment. "I don't think it's easy for everyone," he said.

"Well, no, not everyone," Jay agreed. "But for a lot of us it is."

Adam sighed. "I don't know. I guess maybe sex isn't as big a deal for us. It doesn't always have to *mean* something. It can just be fun."

"Are you saying what we just did meant nothing to you?" said Jay. "Are you saying you *used* me?" He pretended to cry.

"I used you and you liked it," Adam said in a mock-fierce tone. "Now knock it off, or I'll use you again."

Jay reached over, took Adam's hand and laid it on his own chest, their fingers interlocked. Adam felt Jay's heartbeat beneath his palm.

"I'm actually being serious," Jay said. "I know this sounds weird, but I find it easier to fuck a guy than to be friends with him."

"That's because when you don't know anything about him, he can be anything you want," said Adam.

"It sounds like you've thought about this before," Jay said.

"You know how it is," said Adam. "Sometimes you wake up in the middle of the night, find yourself lying beside someone whose name you can't remember, and you have to ask yourself how you got there."

"I almost always know how I got there," said Jay. "What I'm usually thinking about is how I'm going to get away before he wakes up."

That answers that question, Adam thought. He decided that Jay was giving him a hint, and he decided to make it easy for him. "I should probably take a shower," he said. "Do you want one?"

"You go ahead," said Jay.

Adam got up and padded to the bathroom. He stayed in the shower long enough to give Jay a chance to leave, then got out and returned to the bedroom. When he entered he was surprised to find Jay in bed, propped up against the pillows and reading a book. Adam peered at the cover. It was a battered paperback copy of *Jane Eyre.*

"I hope you don't mind," Jay said without looking up. "I

saw it in your bookcase, and since we were talking about it…"

Adam stifled a grin. "I don't mind at all," he said. "What do you think of it so far?"

"It's hard to say," said Jay. "So far all they've done is wander around in some leafless shrubbery, whatever the fuck that is. I thought the whole point of shrubbery was that it had leaves."

Adam got in on the other side of the bed. "It gets better," he said.

"When does madwoman Bertha make her grand entrance?" Jay asked.

"Oh, not for quite some time," said Adam. "But trust me, it's worth it."

Jay shut the book. "I think you're just saying that to trick me into reading this," he said.

"Are you calling me a liar?" said Adam.

"I don't know you well enough to know if you're a liar or not," Jay answered. "With that accent you'd make a great one, but something tells me you don't have it in you."

Adam lifted one eyebrow. "I don't know if I should be offended or flattered," he said.

Jay leaned over and kissed him. "You'll have to decide for yourself," he said. "But for the record, I meant it as a compliment."

Adam arranged his pillows and settled in. Reaching over, he turned off the light on the nightstand on his side. To his surprise, Jay stayed where he was, opened the book, and resumed reading. A full two minutes passed before he looked over and saw Adam watching him.

"Is the light bothering you?" he asked. "I can turn it off."

"It's fine," Adam said.

He didn't know what to make of this man in his bed. They'd known each other only a few hours, but already he felt as if they'd been together for years. He knew somehow that when he closed his eyes he would fall asleep without worry. In fact, the idea of Jay staying beside him, reading, comforted him. He turned on his side, facing Jay, and threw one arm over Jay's middle. Jay rested the book against Adam's arm. Beneath the sheet, one of his feet rubbed along Adam's in casual, familiar touch.

I don't know what this is or what it's going to be, Adam thought as he shut his eyes. *But I like the way it feels.*

SECOND CHANCES

Erin McRae and Racheline Maltese

On the long list of stupid things Pete has done in his life, he's pretty sure none of them are more egregious than answering the door for a date in his shirtsleeves while covered in olive oil and lube. His hands are so slippery, he can barely even turn the knob. He laughs, and then hates himself a little for the dirty internal monologue he can't avoid. Especially considering his wedding ring is still on and apparently not coming off anytime soon.

"Oh my god," Isaac says when he sees him. Pete has to hold the door open with his elbow. "What are you *doing*?"

Pete looks rather sheepishly at his hands. "Um, I was trying to do a thing and it didn't really work," he mumbles and feels grateful that Isaac, while appalled, is still interested enough in him or his bad choices to follow him inside.

"Actually, can you grab some paper towels?" Pete asks, pointing at a cabinet under the sink as he leads the way to the kitchen. "I finished the roll I had out, and I'm trying not to make everything worse. Mostly."

"You did actually remember we had a date tonight, right?" Isaac asks, like he doesn't think Pete is anything worse than flighty.

"Yeah," he says, a little miserably, as Isaac digs the paper towels out from the cupboard and sets them on the counter. "I was trying to get my ring off."

Isaac pauses in the act of shrugging off his coat. "Really?" he asks, surprise in his voice.

"Yeah," Pete laughs ruefully. "It didn't want to come off."

"I can see that," Isaac says dryly.

"Help me with it?"

"Are you sure?" Isaac asks, suddenly cautious.

"It's not like Walter's gonna come back from the grave and do it for me. I mean if he could, we wouldn't be having this conversation."

"Okay, is this you trying to be sweet or just being really, *really* morbid?"

Pete shrugs. "Yes?"

Three years isn't long enough to have gotten used to the idea that his husband is dead, but it's been long enough to develop some fairly fierce coping mechanisms. Facing reality head-on, and speaking the truth of loss aloud, helps. At the least, it keeps him from retreating to a bubble of fantasy and denial.

Isaac chuckles nervously. "Okay then." He sets his jacket down on the counter, far away from the mess Pete's made. Then he starts unbuttoning his shirt.

"Whoa, what are you doing?" Pete asks, as Isaac shrugs the shirt off and drapes it over his jacket.

"You got really gross, slippery shit not ever meant to be used in combination all over yourself *and* your house and we haven't even fucked yet. I'm leaving my nice date-clothes over here before I join you in your bad choices," Isaac says, amused, like it was an actual question and not an exclamation of nervous enthusiasm.

"Sorry," Pete says contritely. He certainly doesn't *want* Isaac deciding to put off the fucking further.

After all, it's why Pete wants to get the ring off in the first place. They've been taking things deliberately—not *slowly*, because that makes them sound like they're in some kind of daytime drama, which they certainly are not. And while it's been driving them both crazy in the best way, they're old enough to be aware their lives are both hot messes and that taking care of their hearts is the kindest thing they can do for each other.

"It's okay," Isaac reassures him, clearly working not to laugh. "Just not on my shirt."

"Yeah. Yeah I noticed that part," Pete says, reaching for him.

"Hey. Hands. Gross." Isaac asks, stepping back out of range.

"But skin." Pete protests.

Isaac, what with the camping-gear store and the outdoor-siness, clearly does not consider the bare skin a big deal. His body's fantastic, and just this side of intimidating to Pete; it reminds him of just how big of a gap there is between being Isaac, the guy who founded a hot new outdoor-gear brand, and himself, the guy who works for the ad agency Isaac hired.

Isaac chuckles. "Yes, skin. Okay, up on the counter."

Pete obeys mutely, trying to hop up next to the sink but almost sliding off and onto the floor when his slick hands slip on the countertop.

Isaac catches him, or tries to, which is all sorts of hot until it's a mess of lost balance and slipperiness *everywhere*.

Eventually Pete gets seated on the counter with Isaac standing between his knees. It makes this disaster of an evening seems like the best plan he's ever had.

"Why tonight of all nights to get creative with the lube?" Isaac mutters, tearing off a paper towel and grabbing Pete's wrist to keep him still so he can get at the worst of the mess. While the concept was sound, not being able to get a firm grip on anything is not going to get that ring off.

"Timing seemed right," Pete says with a shrug.

"Yeah?" Isaac glances up at him through the dark corkscrew curls now tumbling into his face. "Oh my *god,* what did you even do? This stuff is congealing."

"I don't have work tomorrow, and you don't have Jess this weekend?" He says. It both does, and does not, answer the question.

"Oh. Oh *really*," Isaac grins, catching on.

Pete really wants to kiss him, and he would if he were sure he could manage to lean forward without falling off the counter or getting more stuff all over both of them.

"Mmmm." It had been an *awesome* plan. Until the ring hadn't come off.

"The olive oil was your first mistake," Isaac informs him. "Shoulda used Windex"

"Really?" Pete says, wrinkling his nose.

"Yeah. It's slipperier. And like, clean and doesn't get *everywhere?*"

"How do you even know that? Please tell me your ring got stuck too."

"Nope. I mean I took it off all the time for camping and shit."

"What'd you do with it?" Pete asks curiously as Isaac finishes wiping off the mess and goes back to the cupboard looking for his cleaning supplies.

"The day the divorce was finalized I hiked up Rattlesnake Ledge. And I chucked it off the top."

"You did not."

"I completely did."

"It's your wedding ring!"

"Was. And Chad is a fucking asshole. It probably hit someone."

Pete cracks up. He's met Isaac's ex-husband once, at one of Jessica's school concerts. And while he's willing to respect any human being Isaac was married to that long and had a child with, Chad is totally a fucking asshole.

The Windex doesn't actually help matters, which Isaac takes as a personal affront. Pete's hand is likely too swollen at this point for anything to work, but now he's invested, and a valiant attempt is still required.

"Okay, so just to be clear and I don't *need* to mean anything by this, where are you on the dinner, drinks, sex stuff, if we can't get this thing off?" Isaac asks, focusing on the ring, even though he's pretty sure it's not going anywhere.

"He died *three years ago*," Pete points out.

"Yeah, and you're still wearing his ring."

"It seemed weird not to take it off."

"Well, it's gotten pretty weird trying to take it off," Isaac says.

This is the sort of dumb situation that makes him feel like he should give in to Pete's agency's suggestion that he have a blog to personalize the brand. Among other things, he'd be able to enjoy maximum public humiliation.

"Are you annoyed?" Pete asks.

Isaac shakes his head. "Only at the universe. Just like yesterday."

Pete gives him a weak smile.

"So shitty comedies and booze until we cry or..." It's not

meant to be a lead-in, it's just hard to normalize what's an explicitly abnormal situation, and he has no idea what it's legitimate to expect.

"Or you could kiss me."

"Okay, are you…"

"I'm not a child and I'm not drunk, and dear god, we've kissed before," Pete says.

"So this would be the wrong time to point out that you are now covered in olive oil, lube *and Windex!*"

"Unless that's working for you?"

Isaac laughs disbelievingly.

Pete reaches out a hand and, completely not caring what he gets in anyone's hair, grabs the back of Isaac's head and drags him into the kiss.

Isaac has to go up on his toes to make it work, which he does before it occurs to him to protest the mess, and by then it's way too late.

Pete grins at him as he deliberately drags his fingers through Isaac's hair.

Isaac reaches up and catches his wrist, bringing it around to hold between them.

Pete folds their fingers together, and Isaac stares down at his hand and the wedding ring gleaming on it. Pete's worried he's going to ask again if it's okay or if he's sure and now that he is, it just seems so tedious. But Isaac only looks up at him and presses a kiss to Pete's knuckles.

It's terribly sweet and completely scary. It's been a long time since he's been with anyone, and in a way he's almost glad the ring is stuck so he doesn't have to do it alone.

When the moment snaps, they reach for each other's face simultaneously. Pete leans forward on the counter precariously until Isaac shoves him back roughly against the wall, almost banging his head on the corner of a cabinet in the process.

The kiss that ensues is messy and overeager, more teeth than anything else. It's hard to complain when the whole purpose of waiting has been—other than avoiding getting their crazy all over each other—to see if eventually they would get to the place where they just couldn't wait anymore.

Apparently, that place looks like Isaac grinding the heel of his hand against the bulge in Pete's jeans while he pulls back to watch him moan.

"Do you give a shit if we do this here?" Isaac asks, elbows down on the counter now so that he's eye-level with Pete's cock.

Pete shakes his head and throws up his hands a little help-lessly. If he doesn't give a shit about the ring, or the state in which he answered the door, he certainly doesn't give a shit about christening the kitchen counters in his sad little widower apartment where he's never fucked anyone.

"Oh thank god," Isaac says, mostly to himself, as he eases Pete's zipper down.

His cock is thick and heavy in his hands. When he peers up at Pete through his eyelashes and sees him looking back at him in wonderment, it seems ridiculous to have yet another conversa-tion about safety. There are plenty of ways they can hurt each other. Disease, in light of their individual messes after the ends of their marriages, doesn't seem likely.

Still he waits too long, because Pete eventually tips his head to the side and breathes, "Go on then."

Maybe it's because it's been months since his one disastrous post-divorce hookup, but Pete's dick is perfect in his mouth. A little too thick and not too long, and he can get down to the root with just enough of the suggestion of choking to make it really hot.

Pete curses above him. Isaac remembers that it's really hard to smirk with a dick in his mouth, which definitely counts as a good problem to have.

He kneads at Pete's thighs, pushing them as far apart as they'll go in the too-tight jeans. He doesn't want to stop to deal with their clothes, and is grateful when Pete gets both his hands in his hair and makes it clear he's not going anywhere.

Isaac does manage to snake a hand up under Pete's shirt to the flat of his belly. The hair there is short and scratchy, clearly growing in from being waxed. Pete's such an ad man, it's ridiculous. It's a completely different type of vain from that of the guys who work in his shop who define their attractiveness by how likely their hobbies are to get them killed.

Pete's muscles jump. Isaac runs a finger lightly up his side to see if he really is ticklish and is rewarded with a squirm that's a clear yes, and a sharp tug to his hair that's a bit of a scold.

"Just suck," Pete says.

Isaac slaps his hands to Pete's thighs and pulls off.

"No," he says, because he likes a challenge and hopes Pete does too.

Pete just whines and grabs for his own cock.

"Fuck that's hot," Isaac says, and he's tempted just to let it end like this, right here, with Pete jerking off into his face while sprawled awkwardly on the kitchen counter.

Pete stares at him and reaches for the buttons on his shirt. He means to undo them one by one, all sex and confidence, but his hands are clumsy with pleasure and the mishaps with the ring have in no way improved his dexterity. The porn movie moment in his head doesn't quite translate to reality.

"Come on," Isaac says, impatient then, grabbing his hips and tugging him toward the edge of the counter. "Show me your bedroom."

* * *

It takes forever to get there between the kissing and the groping and the being hard, and Pete not bothering to get his pants all the way on or all the way off. But the journey is a lot more fun and a lot less fraught for the trouble.

The room is neat and tidy, hunter green and cream, with a cozy seaside inn sort of vibe. Isaac can't help but glance at the bedside table to see if there's a framed picture of the dead husband. There isn't, and he wonders if it's in a drawer. They've talked about it a lot, and it's not a shadow he's uncomfortable with, but there's probably a difference between the abstraction of it, and the day-to-day reality of Pete's life.

"You can study the room later," Pete says, giving up on his shirt buttons and just yanking the thing over his head. "And even root through my medicine cabinet—"

"I wasn't—"

"You were, and if you want to see a picture of Walter all you have to do is ask, but I would like us to fuck first, because this has been hard won and stupid and we're *here*, and I don't think you know how fragile that is, man-who-throws-his-wedding-ring-off-a-fucking-mountain."

"Chad's really an ass."

"And you still get to miss him," Pete says, finally shucking off the rest of his clothes. He pulls back the blankets on the bed and tumbles in.

Isaac doesn't want to argue, so he shrugs almost bashfully as he thumbs the button on his jeans.

Once they're pressed skin to skin all the reasons this has always been a bad idea—from the dead husband to the messy divorce and the teen daughter, and with the bonus complication of their professional relationship—seem irrelevant.

It's like the first breath of clean air after fire or water, and it feels so good just to revel in it, that at first they have no real purpose beyond touch. Pete is happy to drag his bottom lip over every inch of Isaac's body he can get to while Isaac twists under the attention. Eventually, a few mumbled *what do you want*s and some very distracted answers later, they manage to get it together.

There's lube—and no anticipated dead husband picture—in the bedside drawer, and Isaac is glad to use it for its intended purpose as he shoves Pete's knee up and presses two fingers into him. Pete stares at him wide-eyed, one hand pressed over his mouth, the other working his cock, and Isaac can't look away.

Isaac'll get his cock inside Pete, eventually, maybe even in the morning, but for now, this is more than enough as he grinds against Pete's leg and urges him on.

He even bats the hand away from Pete's mouth.

"I want to hear you," he says, but Pete puts it back, over and over again, until Isaac pins him down with his free hand. Pete arches into it in a way that's a completely delightful tell.

"We're going to have so much fun together," Isaac purrs.

Pete laughs. "Already are."

It's Isaac who comes first, amid a litany of how slick and hot and tight Pete feels around his fingers, and how good it feels to hold him down and on the edge of almost. His cock pulses against Pete's side as he comes, and after everything this night has been it almost doesn't seem messy enough.

Pete agrees and mumbles something nearly incoherent about how Isaac has to come *all* over him next time, before he finally finishes, spurting over his own fingers, with a laugh. Isaac is barely able to ease his fingers out of Pete before they collapse on top of each other and find sleep.

* * *

In the morning, Isaac wakes up to Pete fidgeting with his wedding ring. It's no longer on his finger; instead, Pete is tossing it gently from palm to palm, staring at it like he's never quite seen it before.

"It came off?" Isaac's voice is still rough with sleep and brain not much better.

"Yeah."

"How'd you do it?"

Pete shrugs. "Woke up, tugged. Came off. Guess I needed to get laid."

"Is it weird?" Isaac asks, because less specific is less awful.

"I don't know," he says with a little bit of wonderment. "I suppose I'll freak out eventually. Not right now though."

"Why not now?" Isaac asks, perhaps too fondly. He really likes Pete, maybe more than he should on the traditionally too-easily-misleading morning after. But Pete is sweet and brittle and strange.

"I'm surrounded by good things," Pete says. "Why freak out when they're not gone?"

FUNNY PAPER

Craig Cotter

Robert was taking a history class, and reading about Hitler. Soon after the class started he began texting me Hitler quotes.

I'd set my phone to play the first notes of "Midnight Rambler" for his texts. I decided to text KJ: *Baby*

He hit back immediately: *Hey*

Play?

Yeah OK u come here.

Text address

KJ lived in an apartment in Culver City adjoining Marina Del Rey not far from the ocean. Three 1950s aqua-green two-story buildings in a *C* shape, with a courtyard in the middle with grass, jade plants, palm trees—the usual L.A. fare. The top-floor apartments were bowed-out at an angle. All the apartments had floor-to-ceiling windows in their living rooms.

I walked up the stairs that were flat slabs of concrete and stones set into metal frames and knocked on 2A.

He answered the door in jeans, white ankle socks and a T.

It was eighty-one degrees and I'd traded in my jeans for baggy cotton shorts. I saw a pile of shoes on a mat beside the door and kicked my flip-flops there and walked in.

"What you want to drink?" KJ asked, as I followed him into the kitchen. His hair never seemed to be combed or in any particular pattern. It looked both slept on and made up. It seemed to be cut at many different angles that provided for many different types of hairstyles. Some draped over his ears, some onto his shoulders, some stood up on end—all shiny black. I wondered if it was soft or held in place with mousse or gel.

"Evian looks good," I said.

He handed me a plastic bottle. "You know it's got a huge carbon footprint," he said, smiling. "Shipped from France in a petroleum bottle."

"Why you have it?" I was looking into his big brown eyes.

"Noticed you had a bottle the last time we got Thai," he said.

I followed him into his bedroom, which contained a queen bed and nightstands on each side. Each had a silver bendable metal lamp on it. He set his drink (looked like vodka and cranberry again) on one of the nightstands; I put my water on the other. We sat cross-legged in front of each other.

"So...you're a billionaire," he said with a smile. I could smell marijuana coming through the window from the alley outside and hear teenagers laughing, then silent; then laughing, then silent.

"So...you heard."

"Everyone heard, bro." Now the talk from the alley was deep and serious but I still couldn't make out a word—just a dull rumble. Birds chirped high, stoned teenagers mumbled low. Car noises in the background as just about everywhere in L.A. "You wanna fuck me?"

I like direct talk about sex. I like not playing around. I like to know what guys want, and for them to ask me what I like. But something felt funny with KJ. I felt embarrassed being sexually direct with him and wasn't sure what this was about. Though earlier I'd texted him not to wear deodorant.

I tried to get into my usual flow of being honest but was having trouble with what to say. "All things, Bach things," a voice seemed to say from the alley.

"I've never fucked anyone yet," I told him. "Have you?"

"No."

"A girl?"

"No."

"It always seems weird to think about," I said. "Like when I watch porn, or watch a guy fucking me, he's like really into it. Like he really wants to do that thrusting. I kinda don't get that feeling. It seems weird."

"Yeah," he said, and he started to rub my knee.

"Have you ever been fucked?" I asked him.

"No. I haven't done much yet."

"You wanna fuck me?"

"No. Seems weird to me too."

"Wanna rub each other's feet?" I asked.

He nodded yes and I went back into his living room. I put a pillow on one side of the couch, and then another one on his side. I lay down on my back with my head propped up against a pillow, and told him to lie on the other side. Our legs crossed and my feet were on his chest, and his were near my face with his knees bent. We wiggled to get into a comfortable position, and I took one of his long feet in both my hands and started rubbing each toe. One of his hands held my left ankle, and with his other large hand he started to run long strokes up the sole of my foot.

I could feel his cock through his jeans, and my cock immediately got hard the first time his leg brushed it.

"I can't afford to be shoot hairy everyone," a voice from the alley said. "Mickey said I help you," and then another guy laughed.

"Take off your shirt," I told KJ, and he pulled it off. I'd switch between looking at him and closing my eyes while massaging his feet.

I got in that strange relaxed state where you're hard but you don't want to do anything sexual—you don't need to.

KJ got up, took off his jeans and we found another position with our legs crossing each other. He pulled my feet closer to his mouth and started to lick under my toes. He'd rub my toes under his nose. I stopped rubbing his feet for a while.

He tried to put four of his fingers between all of my toes, but his fingers were too large and my toes were too small.

He pulled himself up to sitting and then folded himself down on me. He put his head under my chin and I stroked his hair. I put my nose in his hair—the smell made my cock throb more and also made me deeply relaxed. We started to make out. His lips are thick. He licked my upper lip under my nose, then pushed his tongue in my mouth.

He knelt on the floor beside the couch and started to suck me. Then he pulled a condom out of his jeans pocket and put it on my cock. "You're gonna fuck me on my bed," he said. He walked into his bedroom and lay flat on his stomach with his legs spread a little. I spread his legs more and kneeled between them. I held the tip of the lubricated condom against his asshole and started to push in. I lay on top of him with my arms under his chest, then holding his shoulders.

I started to fuck, but I knew I didn't have the rhythm. The motion felt artificial. He was moaning, and I was wondering if I was doing it right.

"Ain't no water…" the voice in the alley said followed by more jumbled words.

I was close to cumming and pulled out and came in the condom with my cock between his asscheeks. I lay on top of him for a few seconds and wondered what he was thinking. I rolled off and lay on my side. When he rolled onto his side I saw he'd cum on the blanket. We were facing each other and he pulled me into him, this time with my head under his chin. We hugged each other and fell asleep.

I woke up first about an hour later, afternoon sun still streaming in through the wood blinds. I moved away to look at KJ. His hair had been soft, and was now in a different arrangement. I was wondering what you asked for to get it cut at so many different angles. I liked that it was unpredictable. I looked at his waist that curved a bit before his hips—very much like a girl. He had an hourglass shape down his sides. I looked at his small cock.

When he opened his eyes five minutes later I wondered what he thought of me as a top. Maybe I was totally lame. He sure didn't get a power-fucking like jock boys deliver. But I wanted him to say it was okay.

"Kinda fucking weird, huh?"

"No, it was good," he said.

I felt relieved and didn't feel small. I was generally pissed that I was still five-seven. Some of my hookups used to put one hand around my biceps, touching their fingers, enjoying how I had no muscles. Some of their cocks were thicker than my wrists. Although I liked that they were into me, I didn't want them to think I was a girl. I wanted to grow and get more muscles and feel masculine. I didn't want to play sports anymore or fuck girls, but I wanted to look like I could.

KJ was the first guy I'd played with who wasn't a jock and who looked as fem as me.

"Did you like being a top?" he asked.

"Yeah, it was cool—but it felt weird too. Like I didn't know how to fuck," I said and smiled. "It's like you have to learn that action, it's not natural—it's not genetic," I said with a laugh in the last word.

The boys I had been with—I wondered if they had to learn how to fuck or if it came naturally?

I got crazy horny again looking at KJ, and moved on my side and started to suck him. My cock was by his face and he leaned over and we 69ed on our sides.

"Midnight Rambler" chords. I pulled the phone out of my jeans. Robert had sent me another weird Internet page about an Austrian baker making Nazi-themed cakes.

I texted KJ: *Play?*

Twenty minutes later he texted: *Yeah, here or u?*

Come here

'K, what time?

4:15

'K, cool

Can you wear your black-and-white high-tops?

Sure lol

I beeped KJ in the gate and cracked my front door open. He knocked as he pushed it open and came in.

"Awesome," I smiled, looking down at his tennies. Such long legs and his jeans fit loosely on his hips. Another loud T-shirt, and that black hair that smells so good going all over.

"Any gel or mousse?" I asked.

"None."

"I forgot to ask you about no deodorant."

"I didn't wear any."

"Hot."

"An Absolut Cape Cod, bitch!" he said, smiling.

I loaded it down with four ounces. I grabbed an Evian for myself.

He sat in a blue, fluffy leather chair that was kinda like the one in my dad's study. I lay on the couch, propping myself up with a throw pillow, facing him.

"Thought you were gonna be naked with your ass in the air when I walked in," he said.

"You didn't ask. Next time if you want. 'Cept I might have to make a movie of Daryl and me so you'll know how to tap it," I said to him still smiling. I noticed how much I was smiling. It made my face muscles hurt. Then I thought maybe that would offend him, and I shouldn't have said it.

"I don't know if it would help. You're probably right about the lessons. I don't have a clue about how to fuck ass. Or girls. I like all the massage and sucking and kissing."

"Throw me one of your tennis shoes," I said.

He untied one and tossed it at me. Then he took off the other one and set it on the carpet by the chair. I played with the tennis shoes in both hands as we talked, sometimes smelling inside.

"So you like the foot play?" I asked him.

"Yeah. Had no idea it would feel good. Now I think about it a lot," he said with that big smile with his straight white teeth.

The jocks I'd been with had always taken the initiative, which is something that really relaxed me. I had no moves for initiating sex. I thought this, plus two bottoms, was meaning things wouldn't last long for KJ and me.

"Come over," I said. He walked over and lay on top of me. Maybe initiating wasn't that hard? I wrapped my arms around his back and he buried his face into my hair between my shoulder and neck. I shifted my body left a few inches so he could lie on his side next to me on the couch. His body naturally slid into the opening.

The smell of his hair and skin deeply relaxed me and got me hot like no other guy's had.

"Take me to the bedroom," I said.

He got up, I jumped on his back and he carried me into the bedroom.

"You're supposed to kiss me, or squeeze my ass or put my hand on your cock," I told him, smiling again. I noticed how often we smiled at each other, which was totally weird, nothing I'd done with anyone else. I liked being silly once in a while, being campy, teasing—if a part of me wondered when it was going to end, the message was no longer making it to my conscious mind.

He put my hand on his jeans over his cock, put his hand on my ass and pulled me toward him and kissed me.

"That how it's supposed to go?" he teased.

"Yeah, it's too much pressure to initiate; I got you in the bedroom and didn't like the feeling." (Still smiling as I talked to him...) "Your average baseball player jock really knows how to go for it without much language. Very rough. And you have to hold me," I said, "because I'm smaller. It doesn't work the other way."

He jumped into bed under the covers. I pulled the covers back, jumped in front of him, then quickly pulled the covers back over us. He pulled me close.

"You learn pretty fast," I told him. "Maybe you're morphing into a top."

We were both in our clothes, and he stroked my side above my T-shirt and shorts.

He put the side of his head against me, his lips just over my ear, and said, "I think I can get us going, if you want that, and tell you shit to do." His head dropped back on a pillow and he squeezed me softly with his arms. I grabbed his right hand and, interlacing our fingers, put it on my stomach. I could feel his hard on against my shorts.

"But the fucking part of top," he said quietly, "I don't think I can do it. I've never wanted to fuck."

"'S'all right." I played with his large hand. Fingers long and strong. Big smooth nails. This boy is a god.

"How much you like getting fucked?" he asked.

"The first time I thought it was impossible. I was on my stomach and he was on top of me. When I told him to stop he whispered in my ear, 'This your first time?' When I said, 'Yeah,' he slowed down and started kissing my neck. And then I relaxed. It was great the first time. I had no idea it could feel so good."

"I like all the other stuff better," KJ said.

"How do you know if you never tried top?"

"I didn't know feet were good until you. And I never knew I'd like getting rimmed or rimming until you." He shifted his body so more was against me.

Silence for a few minutes. Guys not talking can be a real turn-on. I learned not to be embarrassed about my own silences like I learned how not to be embarrassed to ask questions. I think I learned both by third grade.

"But I don't want to fuck you, and I don't want you to fuck me again," he said.

I wondered what was wrong.

"But the rest we do—I really like it," he said. He put his big hand under my shorts, inside my briefs. I was hard and he played with my balls and squeezed my hard-on. "So I'll be the one to get us started from now on. And you can introduce anything new that's not fucking," he said.

"How about my purple dildo?" I said.

"No problem as long as you don't try to fuck me with it or want me to put it in you," he said, and he squeezed me hard.

"You're a freak, KJ."

"We're both freaks, you little fag," he said, and put his nose in my ear.

THE KINGDOM OF HAEVEN

Eric Andrews-Katz

He could hear them. Whispered words in hushed voices that sank into long moments of silence. A hissing sound slithered through like an invisible serpent followed by a brief beeping noise. Then heavy silence before the cycle continued. Subtle movements of shadows shifted in the darkness without any distinguished formations.

"Are you ready?" a voice asked from the darkness.

"Yes," came the solemn reply.

A red light flickered from somewhere in the corner, but no one turned to look.

"I love you, Tyler," a frantic voice whispered. "Tyler?"

He felt fingers entwining his own. Comfortable, strong and familiar sensations transferred through the simple squeezing of his hand.

A high-pitched sound rang out, thundering from the darkness and exploding brightly, momentarily blinding him with light. Then blackness. Another voice faintly calling. It softly beckoned him, barely audible and quickly fading. He heard his name and felt the gentle touch on his arm.

"*Tyler...*

"*Tyler...*

"*Tyler...*"

"Tyler." The gentle shaking continued and the soft voice called to him. "Tyler, wake up."

General Tyler Addicott's eyes fluttered opened to find Captain Wilyem Turrick waking him from his nap. He yawned with a stretch and smiled up at his husband of six years, taking in the wide hazel eyes, clean-shaven cheeks and head, and the full-toothed grin dominating his face.

"Hey, Honey," Tyler said. He looked at the blinking red numbers from the clock on the wall. "How long was I napping?"

Wilyem stopped jostling Tyler's arm and sat on the end of their bed. His hands twitched in his lap and the red tip of his tongue cradled the edge of his front teeth.

"About two hours," Wilyem said. "But that's not important." He stilled himself with great effort and paused for a dramatic silence. "They called."

It took the general a moment to fully comprehend what was being said. He bolted to an upright position. The light blanket fell to his naked waist exposing his broad shoulders, with a trimmed layer of downy hair crossing his chest. Tyler reached out, taking Wilyem's hands into his own.

"What'd they say?" he demanded.

"Only that they wanted to see us both in the Royal Chambers within two hours."

"That doesn't necessarily mean anything," Tyler replied, trying to keep control of his eagerness. Wilyem's excitement was contagious, and he felt his chest tightening with anticipation.

"Except," Wilyem said, his grin slowly expanding. "Conclave broke an hour ago and the Badge is being shown."

Tyler followed the nudge from Wilyem's head to the pulled shades. Throwing off the covers he leapt from the bed and ran naked to the window. He peeked through the blinds and saw Haeven's purple insignia projected from the tower of Ravaggio Palace. From the distant hilltop the encircled silhouettes of two men, back-to-back with arms linked at the elbows, illuminated the Aresium dome that protected the capitol city from the toxicity of the planet's atmosphere.

"It still doesn't mean that I've been chosen," Tyler said, turning back to his partner.

"I'd say it does!" Wilyem answered. Standing up, he strode over to the window and embraced his partner who was seven years his senior. He let his hands move over Tyler's strong hips, sliding around his back to give the firm buttocks a playful swatting.

"Hail to the new King of Haeven!" Wilyem declared, placing his lips on his husband's mouth.

Tyler gave in to the kiss's passion before stopping.

"You don't know that," Tyler said, his breathing coming harder. His bottom lip trembled with excitement and his penis pressed against the front of Wilyem's uniform. "You're gonna jinx my chances."

"I'm forty-three and don't believe in jinxes. You know you got it," Wilyem said, pulling Tyler closer to him by the small of his back. "Who else are they going to elect, General Smyth?"

"Don't underestimate Ronald," Tyler protested. "He's a formidable army man."

"Maybe," Wilyem said, slapping Tyler's butt. "But you're better." He withdrew his arms, returning to his seat on the bed's edge. "Everyone knows that General Smyth has the social skills of a crater slug, and about the same emotional range. He doesn't know how to express himself other than barking out orders at anyone within earshot. No one likes him enough to elect him king."

"There have been worse kings of Haeven," Tyler answered, playing devil's advocate. "And they could choose General Stolzer, or Lozzi or half a dozen others."

"They could," Wilyem said. "But you and I both know they won't. Stolzer's Bisexual Support campaign hurt his political career too much to make him a serious candidate, and Lozzi? Get real. He's still an Earth sympathizer and that's not going to get him elected. There's no one else that compares to your service record and charisma. It has to be you that they've chosen!"

"We better get going if we're going to find out," Tyler said. "I'll get cleaned up if you schedule the Magno."

"Already done," Wilyem said showing off his proudest smile. The even teeth showed through full lips on a rounded face. He winked, allowing a boyish quality to settle on his cheeks. "And I made sure it was a seated car. The future king isn't arriving for his coronation in a common standing booth."

"You know," Tyler said. "I love you more than the Great Rivers of the Svenson."

"Then I'm a lucky, lucky man!" Wilyem answered. "Get ready. The clock is blinking away."

"Do you remember your arrival on the planet?" Tyler muttered as the car-pod raced past the Docking Center. The building was well lit, signaling a recent arrival of men from Earth.

The two officers sat with their hands clasped together, hanging down between their reclined seats, and looking out the sides of the clear pod: their usual positions when riding the

Magno together. A gentle hissing sounded as enriched oxygen was pumped into the car.

"It's been twenty-five years and I still remember the fear and the excitement of finally being in Haeven."

"Fear?" Wilyem playfully scoffed. "I couldn't wait to get here. I had the money together before I turned of age. I spent my twenty-fifth birthday at the Center for Relocation and was *so* ready to go! After all the restrictions and overpopulation issues the POGS created..."

"Wilyem!" Tyler reprimanded the usage of the vulgar vernacular.

"Sorry," he said unapologetically. "The Pro-Populationists if you'd rather. I don't know why any self-respecting Queer person would *want* to stay back on Earth."

"You don't think we've created another ghetto?" Tyler asked. "But on a planetary scale?"

"You're crazier than a Saturn moth!" Wilyem said. He stared incredulously at Tyler's rectangular face, squared jaw and angled nose. The longer spiked hair on top still showed a rich chestnut color, but the shorn sides of his head glistened with silver. "They depleted the natural resources by overpopulation and expelled all Queer people as a solution. It's ironic that in a hundred and fifty years the two gender specific satellites have become prosperous, independent nations. Let Lozzi whine about reconciliation with Earth; I say the only purpose that planet serves is sending their gay men here, and their women to Minervite."

"Well," Tyler said. "You always were a chauvinist."

"And soon," Wilyem said with a wink. "It'll be Mr. Regent Chauvinist."

"By the Four Suns!" Tyler said with a rolling of his eyes. "You probably have the business card already picked out. You do know there's no real power that goes with that title, right? It's just an honorary position for the Husband of the King. And that's only *if* I get elected, mind you."

"Maybe," Wilyem said with a self-righteous nodding of his head. "But since I won't be eligible for the throne anymore, and will hold the title of regent for as long as you live, I'll make the most of what I can."

"You're incorrigible," Tyler replied, shaking his head. He gave Wilyem's hand a playful squeeze.

"Yes," came the cocky reply.

The car tilted back as it began its climb up Royal Hill. Through the pod's front dome the Ravaggio Palace came into view. Constructed from the planet's natural resource of aresium, the walls were tinted dark russet to make the fortress as private as it was impregnable. The purple emblem of the two men linked at the elbows was still being projected from the Donjon of the castle.

"Identify yourselves," commanded the masculine tone through the intercom.

Both men reached into the side pocket of their chairs to retrieve a pair of goggles and slid them over their heads. The retina scan briefly activated and completed its work. They removed the goggles, returning them to the pockets, and sat back in their seats.

"Welcome General Addicott and Captain Turrick. Regent Torvino is expecting you. Docking connections now complete."

The voice clicked off. Red lights flashed from the panel signaling the Royal Magno Station authorizing their entry, and the car's speed increased with the direct pull toward the palace doors.

Projected by hologram onto the entryway was King Pasqual's official portrait. Above the picture and written in red letters:

To Die Is to Sleep—and We Shall Rise Come Mourning. Below the royal likeness, blazing in red: 3340—3401—And He Shall Be Remembered In the Kingdom of Haeven.

The projection briefly fluttered as the barriers opened. The car flew into the landing dock and waited as the castle doors closed. A loud, serpentine hissing echoed throughout the chamber as the toxic air was cleared away and the car was decontaminated.

"In a few hours," Wilyem stated. "Your picture is going to be up there and it will read Long May He Reign."

"Stop it," Tyler harshly whispered. He wiped his palms on the knees of his uniform. His right leg twitched with undischarged energy. "You're making me nervous."

Wilyem reached across the seat and took Tyler's face in his hands. He looked into the resilient amber eyes, past the strong military bravado, and into the depths of the man behind it all.

"Baby." The endearment was practically whispered. "You got this. You've proven yourself to be a compassionate man, as well as a fair and strong leader. Not since the Infiltration of 3001 has a general earned four stars before the age of fifty, and he wasn't nearly as popular as you. So I've read."

Wilyem leaned in and let their lips touch. He felt the spark that was always there between them. It pulled them closer, and he heard the breath racing through Tyler's nostrils. Wilyem opened his mouth, letting his tongue explore, teasing the edges of Tyler's lips. He felt the general's strong arms wrap around him, locking at the small of his back and resting above the curve of his buttocks.

"I love you very much," Tyler whispered. "You know that, don't you?"

"Yeah, I do." Wilyem's lips twitched into an impish grin. "Your Majesty."

For a brief flash Tyler let his stoic exterior vanish and allowed the hint of giddiness to show through.

"Could you just imagine?" he said with boyish excitement.

"Yes," Wilyem replied. His smile grew when he saw Tyler finally succumbing. "Yes, I can."

The general looked over Wilyem's shoulder, his expression erasing all hints of delighted anticipation.

"We'll know in a short while," Tyler said with a nod. "Here comes the regent."

The two men broke their embrace, turned 'round and snapped into a military stance as the pod doors opened, and Regent Torvino approached. The King's widower was dressed in the uniform of Haeven except that his was black instead of blue, and the insignia was larger and placed central on his chest.

Regent Torvino walked across the silent room, his black boots echoing on the high-polished floor. His hair was gray and thinning at seventy-six, but his uniform was worn well, boasting a toned, stout body and a muscular pair of legs. The salt-and-pepper mustache attractively covered the upper half of a thin pair of lips, and the lights reflected like fiery pinpoints from the corners of his glasses.

"Hail Regent of Haeven!" both men said in unison. They crossed their right hand to their left shoulder and extended the arm with a closed fist in perfect synchronization.

"Hail General Addicott and Captain Turrick," Regent Torvino said. He repeated the salute and all three men lowered their arms.

Tyler leaned forward and whispered. "How you holding up, Cameron?"

Regent Torvino rolled his eyes with a heavy sigh.

"I'm still numb from Randyl's passing," he whispered in a

congested tone. "But glad those bitches in Conclave didn't take too long. I am done with Heads of State."

"Any idea who they've chosen?" Wilyem asked with a mischievous tone.

"Give me a break!" Cameron moaned, shooting him an exhausted look. "Smyth, Stolzer and Lozzi have been yapping at my heels like Gorwich pups since Conclave broke. You will all know soon enough, and I can be excused from my duties."

The regent started off with the two men a step behind him.

"Please tell me it's not that Son-of-a-Praggie Smyth!" Wilyem muttered.

"It's not," Cameron softly confirmed over his shoulder. "And that's all I'm saying."

The three men entered a long hallway with dimmed chandeliers illuminating the way. Precisely hung on either side were photographs, perfectly aligned and running the length of the halls: Haeven's previous line of kings and their regents. Each couple stared out from their Official Portraits, silently offering warnings and advice as the men walked past. On either side there was blank space for future portraits to be added.

"It always takes my breath away," Wilyem said gazing at the pictures. "Seeing all these faces of great men gives me so much pride."

"Ass kisser," Cameron playfully accused out the side of his mouth.

The three men softly chuckled as they entered the Royal Chamber. All sounds were silenced as they walked under the high-vaulted ceilings of the Grand Hall. The regent led the two men down the blue carpet running down the center aisle of the massive room. Although it was built to hold half the planet's population, only the privileged were selected to watch the prestigious event of King Crowning.

The thirteen members of Conclave lined one side, standing in their purple robes with the planet's emblem in black, their cowls hanging loosely over the tops of their faces. At rigid attention on the opposite wall, two-dozen of the highest-ranking military officers stood saluting as the trio passed. The entire room was draped in fervent silence.

"I love you," Wilyem whispered. He reached out and took hold of Tyler's hand, giving it a firm squeeze of confidence. The captain glanced at his husband with an affectionate smile.

Tyler kept his eyes locked forward. His face void of expression, he struggled with keeping his bottom lip from trembling. He was aware of all eyes in the room following them as they walked toward the dais and throne. A wave of vulnerability washed over him, and he did his best to keep his knees from buckling. His hand closed tighter around Wilyem's. The two palms pressed firmly into one another, and General Tyler Addicott found his strength.

The throne was placed centrally on a raised platform three short steps up from the main floor. It pulsed with the dark blue light Aresium gave off in its raw and strongest form. To the left of the stairs stood Generals Smyth and Lozzi, with their respective spouses and several men of their regiments. General Stolzer stood with his spouse on the right side, with a small entourage behind.

"Look at their eyes," Wilyem excitedly whispered. "It says it all."

Regent Torvino reached the end of the aisle and stopped before the steps leading to the throne. Instead of directing them to their position on the right side, he turned sharply around, snapping his heels and saluting.

The two men following came to a sudden halt. Wilyem felt his chest grow tight, but Tyler breathed out long and slow through his lips. Their entwined fingers tightened and with the comfortable, strong and familiar sensations transferred through the simple squeezing of his hand, Tyler found peace and knew his time had come.

"Are you ready?" Wilyem whispered.

"Yes," came the solemn reply.

"Hail!" Regent Torvino shouted with a sudden salute. "Hail to General Tyler Addicott, the Undoubted King of Haeven!"

"Hail to the Undoubted King!" the room thunderously echoed.

Tyler said nothing. As the room erupted with the sound of his name he felt completely paralyzed. The men were all saluting him, their arms jutting out with their fists clenched for strength and support. The general looked around him, a tear forming in his eye at the exaltation of his fellow officers. He looked at Wilyem and saw the look of adulation and love expressed with tears running down his face.

Tyler smiled at the man he loved. He looked over Wilyem's shoulder to see Regent Torvino standing very still and looking quite serious. The regent stepped up the few stairs of the dais until he stood next to the throne. His hand crept forward until his fingertips curled around the chair's tall backing. At his touch the Aresium changed from dark blue to a pale red. The light's silent pulsing slowed until it became a solid color.

No one else seemed to notice.

"I love you, Tyler," Wilyem frantically whispered. He reached for Tyler's hand, bringing it to his lips.

A high-pitched sound rang out, thundering about the Great Hall. A bright light flashed out from the throne momentarily blinding him before fading to instant darkness. The room exploded with the sound of his name.

"Tyler!"

"Tyler...
"*Tyler...*"

Wilyem felt Tyler's hand slowly release its grip. He looked up, eyes full of tears, and saw the machine's red light pulsing slow, stop and flatline. Clinging to Tyler's hand, Wilyem held it to his lips not able to let go. He felt a hand touch his shoulder and looked up from Tyler's hospice bedside. Dr. Cameron Torvino nodded, trying his best to offer what comfort he could.

"He's gone," the doctor compassionately said.

From somewhere behind him in the small bedroom, Wilyem could hear a prayer being whispered.

"*And it shall be said, the time is fulfilled and the Kingdom of Heaven is at hand.*"

MATTERS OF THE HEART

Dale Chase

I can't figure why I'm so gone on Ray Seel. He's not a pretty man—hell, I'm prettier—but he can do the littlest thing, like knock the dust off his hat, and I'm smitten all over again. He's a lean twenty-year-old working the family ranch and I'd never given him much thought until a few months ago when I had to jail him for disturbing the peace. Everything turned that night and I've no idea why.

He and his fellow cowhands were whooping it up in the Palace Saloon where I happened to be wetting my whistle. When a fight broke out, I turned to see Ray punch Elwood Sims, who's too old to be a threat to anybody, so I had to intervene. If Ray had settled down there'd have been no problem, but he was drunk and threw a punch at me so I decked him. I then got him to his feet and marched him to jail. I hated doing this as he's a good kid, but I couldn't be seen favoring somebody who'd struck the marshal. Further manhandling was required when he balked at going into the cell, and I ended up slapping him to get him in line. By the time he was locked up something was afoot in me.

"He was bottom dealing," Ray said as the cell door slammed. "I called him on it and he insulted me so I hit him."

"You don't settle things beating on an old man," I said.

He gave no further argument, just wrapped his hands around the iron bars and I was lost for a second, wondering how those hands would feel on me. "Just settle down," I said, stepping back. "You'll stand before the judge tomorrow morning, pay a fine and maybe learn a thing or two. Now get some sleep. Your night is over."

I kept looking in after he dozed off as I was caught up in the sight of him laid out on the cot. Finally I fled to my desk because that something afoot in me was gaining and I had to turn it like drovers do a stampede. In my office I told my deputy, Skip Loudon, "You go out and keep order. I'll take the duty in here."

Skip passed me a look, shrugged and went out. I didn't care what he thought, even as I had no idea what that might be. It was hard enough to figure what I thought. I sat at my desk, but replayed the punches Ray and I had traded along with my shoving him into the cell. The night proved a long one and next morning I stole in once more, hoping to see just what I did which was him lying sound asleep, pants open, hand inside. When I later walked him to the courthouse, I was near beside myself as I felt intimacy when there'd been no such thing. Once he'd paid his fine he fled without so much as a look my way, but this was no bother as I knew his anger would pass, which it did.

Ever since then I've been Ray's captive, only he doesn't know it. It wouldn't look right for the marshal to be seen mooning over a fellow, especially one fourteen years younger, so I go about my peacekeeping here in Silver City, New Mexico, although I may be less patient toward those disturbing that peace. This I attribute to enduring a kind of pent-up swoon.

I've never been good at matters of the heart. Matters of law I know well, but they're set down in books so a man need only consult the proper passage, should a question arise, which it never does. Nobody attempts to set down rules for the heart, leaving it to disturb a man's peace to the point he's all but cooked from a fire he can't put out. Water, coffee, whiskey, none dampen the flame so the man goes around in an awful state, seared inside. Worst of all is him welcoming the agony.

Ray comes to town with two ranch hands every Saturday, relieving me of a long week without him. I bathe on Fridays so I'll be fresh for him though he's got no idea on that. I'm thick in body compared to Ray, but believe I cut a fine figure and besides, a lawman needs strength both in build and character. I'm never more reminded of this, especially the character part, than when I see Ray on Saturday.

He gets in around noon, takes a room with his pards, which I try not to think on, him in drawers in their company, which they surely don't appreciate. They'll go around town, visiting stores to make purchases or just gawk, then hit the ice-cream parlor. I keep a distance, but not so far I don't see him here and there. When they finally go into a saloon I settle some as this is more my territory. Ice-cream parlors are for kids.

Ray has the lanky brown hair of a hundred other men, brown eyes, and the ruddy look of an outdoorsman. He favors blue shirts, red kerchiefs and black wool pants, and his white hat is sweat stained and battered. Why such things stir me I don't know, they just do. I'm always hoping he'll get drunk and tear up some so I'll have to arrest him again, but he's only done it the one time. And I don't know I could stand it now, him stretched out in a cell.

This particular Saturday is hot, it being July. I sweat when not even moving. I find myself restless as I watch men ride into town because it's nearly four and Ray hasn't shown. I'm also annoyed at being restless and when I'm forced to break up a fight spilling from the Grand Saloon, I'm less than patient. It's two local men, good friends who've gotten into a spat, and they take heed when I threaten jail if they don't observe order. It's as they depart in opposite directions that I note Ray Seel riding in. And he's alone.

I stand captured out front of the mercantile, heart beating like I'm running a race, parts lower rising to the occasion. I try not to look, but do. Ray ties his horse at the hotel and I see he's clad not in a blue shirt but a white one and looking like a million bucks, at least to me. I'm struck by his maybe wanting to impress me and I enjoy about ten seconds of swoon before it crosses my mind that he may be dressed up for somebody else.

Appearing casual when the body is running a race all on its own isn't easy, even for a lawman of some repute. I cross the street to a spot where Ray is headed, then run into him like I just happened along. "Ray," I say as he approaches. "How are you keeping? How's your Pa?"

"I'm doing good, Marshal," he replies. "Pleased to have the week past. Pa's well, getting after me like usual."

Arden Seel is a demanding fellow who I'd not want to cross. Big as a bull and just as mean, he often acts no better than his stock, but his cattle operation is a success. If he knew my thoughts toward his son, he'd shoot me.

"I'll have to get out and see him one of these days," I say, not caring a whit for Arden Seel. "Where's your pards?"

"Dan's gone off after some girl and Elmo up and quit. Pa's in a state over that as he's having to do twice the work. I'm lucky to get away at all."

"Let me buy you a drink."

"Much obliged."

Ray is a welcoming sort of fellow, easy and mild, and we settle in at the bar of the Buckhorn Saloon. His voice is smooth as honey and when he pushes his hat back I seize with that torment I've come to crave. "New duds?" I ask when we're on the second whiskey.

"Yep. 'Bout time."

I want to say how fine he looks, but keep my mouth shut as the marshal can't be seen going soft though I'd argue there's some hardness involved. "White shirt will draw dirt faster than blue," I offer which is a silly thing to say but I have to say something.

"Suppose so."

"You staying at Morse House?" I ask.

"Nah. I'm at Brandle's. Cheaper, but it's not much more than a cot in your jail." This comes with a smile that warms me to the point I'm lost for words. I break into a grin and feel the heat of a flush on my face. I find myself embarrassed at the conversation, never mind it's no more than the time of day. Further indulgence is denied me when gunshots are heard. I enjoy another couple seconds of Ray before going out to corral a drunken cowpoke shooting streetlamps. As I crack my pistol over his head, dropping him to a heap, I glance over to see Ray standing out front of the saloon and I'm puffed up beyond reason at him watching me perform my duty. When I march the drunk to jail, I do it with great authority, knowing Ray's eyes are on me.

Later on I take supper and am near done when in walks Ray. Seeing me, he comes over. "Join you?"

"Sure," I say, thrilled at the request, "but I'm about done. I recommend the beefsteak."

He laughs. "Pass. I get enough of that at home." He orders

stew and biscuits. "Quiet night," he offers when he's got his food.

I realize only then I haven't taken a bite since he sat down so I eat some before answering. "Best kind of night. Hope to keep it that way."

"You hear the Benson gang is in the area?"

"I did. Got a wire from Sheriff Dix over in Cochise County saying they'd departed the territory headed east. Skip and I are prepared should they make the mistake of coming here."

"How many men you killed, Marshal?"

The answer is six, but I won't say because I don't believe the law should count notches. "Don't keep track of such things," I answer.

"Which means a good number."

I like the way he gets under my skin, and also don't. The familiar heat stays with me and keeps my blood rushing. Can he possibly know what he does to me?

Soon my food is gone, my coffee cup empty, and I should get back to patrolling the town, but I'm too caught up in Ray who's breaking off pieces of biscuit to sop in his gravy. I can't help but fix on this as, for a smitten man, it's highly arousing. I should get up and go, except I'm hard below and don't want to show it. Wish I had my coat. Damned hot weather. Finally Ray's meal is done, and he sits back to sip his coffee. "Yes sir, a fine night," he declares. "Think I'll play some cards." He stands, puts on his hat, and I then get up, but my hat doesn't go on my head. I hold it to conceal my privates.

"You keep your cool," I advise and I hurry to pay my check and leave. Even away from his company, I'm slow to calm. My hat remains in hand, shielding myself when probably nobody's taking note. Ray then comes out, nodding as he passes. He's all man now, grown up fellow going to drink and gamble. I think on him sitting in at cards and it's as I so indulge that I realize he's left me in bad shape. To remedy this, I go to the privy out back of the Grand Saloon where I free my cock and gain manly release while picturing Ray Seel in a compromising position. Once satisfied, I return to lawman duties.

It's after midnight when shots ring out and I turn to see Ray rush out of the Buckhorn Saloon, jump on his white cow pony and ride from town. I go over to find a stranger dead on the saloon floor, gun still in hand. "What happened?"

"Ray called him out and they both drew," comes the response.

"Who drew first?"

Replies fall into two camps, some saying it was Ray, others saying it was the stranger who they declare a sharp. I give up trying to sort things out. As I head to the livery to get my horse, I run into my deputy. "Ray Seel just shot a fellow dead at the Buckhorn," I say. "I'm going after him."

"You getting up a posse?"

"I can handle this on my own."

Skip passes me another of those looks of his, but I don't bite. "You see to things," I tell him, not waiting for a reply. Soon I'm saddled up and packing rifle and bedroll as a lawman in pursuit has no idea how long he'll be out or what may develop. Still, I find myself in no hurry to get moving. When I finally do it's not full gallop like usual. An easy canter is all I can muster.

It tears me up that I'm after Ray Seel, tears me up to carry my rifle as using it would put more end to me than him. As I ride along I suffer a churning of the innards, wishing he hadn't run because it makes him look guilty. I want him to come to his senses, stop and turn around, but know that's more wishful thinking. He's done about the worst a fellow can do and taken the only road he sees.

He'll either stay on the run till his horse gives out or try to hole up somewhere. I think ahead to hospitable spots, which are few, it being hard country. I ride toward a spring I know, uncertain about catching my prey.

Ray isn't there and it's too dark to read tracks so I take a break and let my horse drink his fill while I stand in moonlight hating what I'm about. Never has my job been a trial. I've always felt born to the law, always upheld every aspect, yet I'm already thinking to maybe let this chase fall away. Stay out long enough to look good, then return to town saying I lost him, which I see will be more truth than I can bear. This gets me back on my horse and on my way because I can't abide Ray being lost to me.

I stop once more, just as dawn comes up, and this time I find tracks that confirm Ray's headed east. A thinking man would have gone west to Arizona where I have no authority, but Ray's not thinking at present. He's scared so he's running. Once my horse and I are rested, both of us taking on water, both emptying of some as well, we're back at it though I still don't press too hard. I plan to keep on the trail, but not burn it up. Ray will wear down at some point and that's how I'll get him, when he's beat in both body and spirit. As I ride along I consider how things will go down, different ways playing before me, none good. I can't believe he'd shoot me, but then I'd never have figured him to shoot anybody. He might try to outwit me in some manner known only to young hotheads, but I have experience on my side and am seldom outwitted.

Around noon I stop at a little Mexican hamlet and, knowing enough Spanish to get by, I learn Ray's had a meal then lit out. "White horse," says a fellow. "Rio Grande," he adds, pointing east, like anybody out here wouldn't know where the big river lies. The good news is Ray didn't change horses. A thinking man would have done that as a horse will usually fail to outrun his owner's trouble. I leave the hamlet after a meal, pressing on until night falls.

I can smell the Rio Grande before I see it, fresh water mingling with flowery scents the land gives off under cover of night. I'm thinking to water my horse, then ride on to Hatch which is the first town on the river, get me a bed and some rest, a good meal, maybe a drink or two. I'll ask around after Ray and pick up pursuit next day.

Having a plan perks me up and I've got my horse turned toward the river when I see a campfire up ahead. Most likely it's a traveler who can't afford a room or some cowpoke bedded down among strays he's rounded up, but, not being sure, I approach with caution. When still some distance I leave my horse and continue on foot. Once close, I see the fire set in front of a rock formation and there beside it lies Ray Seel, sound asleep.

I take great care now, nearing the man I've come to arrest, but I put off my duty in favor of just looking. He appears much as he did back on that cot in my jail only now his saddle is his pillow. One hand rests at his side while the other lies on his chest, gripping his six-shooter. My fingers are on my holstered gun, but I make no move to draw. The lawman part of me says to get on with things and take him unawares, but the man behind the badge wants to throw off that star, throw off everything and draw the boy into my arms. I want to tell him all is not lost and assure him I'm on his side. I want to pet him, maybe kiss him. My dick wakes at such thoughts and I savor the heft. The dog in me won't lie down.

How long I stand watching I don't know, but finally I shake off wishful thinking in favor of doing my job. I draw my gun and enter his camp, then nudge his foot. "Don't move," I say when his eyes open. "I don't want to shoot you. Toss your gun away, easy like."

He makes no move to resist or comply and I get he's thinking on alternatives. "Do it!" I demand. This stops any nonsense and he tosses the gun my way. I slip it into my belt, then take a seat on a big rock. "You can go back to sleep if you want. We'll not head back till daylight."

He looks around like there's an answer hidden in the dark, and when he finds none he looks to me. "How'd you find me?" he asks.

"Your fire. Those of the criminal persuasion know to make a dark camp. Same as they'd know to change horses and keep riding. Same as they'd know to head west to Arizona Territory where I have no authority."

A downcast look comes over him. "You're no criminal, Ray," I tell him, "but running makes you appear one."

"I shot that fellow."

"And he shot as well so there's a chance for you in that."

I know what's next before it comes. "Is he dead?" asks Ray.

"Yes."

"That's a hanging offense."

"Maybe not. I spoke to witnesses who can't say who fired first. Absent clear proof, it'll likely be seen as you shooting in defense of your life."

He sits up and runs a hand through his hair, capturing me again with something that would go unnoticed by anyone but me. I think on my fingers in that hair and maybe somewhere else. "There's no guarantee," he says, breaking the spell.

"Only justice," I reply, "but it usually does well in my town."

"Wish I'd not have sat in with him," offers Ray.

I've no response to this so I turn things another direction.

"Why don't you get some sleep. There's nothing to be gained hashing it over now."

He studies me. "You going to keep an eye on me all night?"

"That I am."

"Won't you need sleep?"

"A lawman learns to do without."

He chuckles which lifts me because he's showing something other than fear. "I need a piss," he says.

"Go ahead, but don't try anything."

He rises, steps over to a creosote bush, opens his pants and sets to business. That he doesn't turn his back is not lost on me, him standing in profile to issue his stream. I get a good look at his equipment and when he's done and shaken off the last, he keeps himself in hand, playing around like he knows I'll enjoy the show. Then he stops, tucks himself away and buttons up. Without a word he lies back down. When he keeps his eyes open, I start to wonder if maybe he does know he gets to me. That could prove dangerous.

"No need to sit up all night, Marshal," he says. "You can stretch out by the fire and still keep your gun on me."

"Thanks, but I'll stay put."

"Suit yourself."

When the fire burns low, I add more branches, which is maybe a mistake as the brighter light seems to stir Ray. He blows out a sigh and slides a hand down to his privates where he commences to prod. "Doubt I can sleep in my present state," he offers. "You know how it is, Marshal, fellow pent up in the manly way."

Not waiting for comment, he undoes his pants. I'm thinking he'll get a hand inside, but he surprises me by pushing everything down around his knees. I'm bushwhacked at the sight and when he starts handling himself, I clamp my jaw to hold back comments rising from the depths. Ray Seel definitely has an idea what he does to me and is looking to trade on it.

He's hard in no time and I recall how that was, stiff more than not. He does everything possible to entice me, pulling and wagging his dick, and when I don't give way he smiles, issues a great sigh, and puts his cards on the table. "You're welcome to join in, Marshal," he says. "Nobody out here but us, nobody to know you set aside your badge. And, as you can see, I'm up for something."

The dog part of me is ready to strip off and give it to him so hard he'll sit his saddle with difficulty, but the lawman part holds out for justice, though the hold is thinning. I ache to set my prick free, but remain seated on the rock, allowing I can at least enjoy the show.

"You know, Marshal, I've always taken note of you," Ray says.

"Have you now."

"You're a notable man and I, for one, don't miss such a thing. You think I'd invite just anybody to share my fire? Or suck my dick?" He stops working himself to point his rod at me and damned if I'm not sorely tempted. He then starts grinding his hips, working me like he's not being held at gunpoint. "I'm in need, Marshal, and I'm thinking you are too."

I haven't yet gotten past him calling me a notable man. Everything else is gravy and what the hell, it's just as he said, we're out in the middle of nowhere, seen only by ourselves. As if he can read my thoughts, he says, "Fuck me, Marshal," and that does it. I stand, holster my gun, then unbuckle my gun belt and set it where I can get to it if need be. I then open my pants and free my cock. "Turn over," I command and he gets onto all fours. I crawl in behind and part his buttocks. "Fuck me," he says again, so I do.

Getting into him is payoff for the torment I've endured these past months. When I commence taking my satisfaction, I can't keep from going full out, which brings the rise way too soon. But no man can hold off nature so I pump it good, spewing into the man I covet, and everything else, laws and rules and courts and every goddamn thing there is, falls away. I carry on throughout, roaring or whooping or whatever you'd call the kind of noise that tells the world a man is having a come. Creatures who've crept close in the dark now scatter and I swear the fire crackles at our heat, but then it's over and I slip out of him and fall to one side. Soon as I do, he rolls onto his back and says, "Now me." I manage to raise up enough to see him still stiff, so I gather what I have left and get my mouth on him, finding need suddenly reborn. Soon I'm sucking him with a fury and getting a mouthful of spunk that I swallow right down.

I keep at him even when he's soft because I want us tethered in some way. I suck his morsel and he moans and runs a hand through my hair. I find myself swooning and savoring that swoon because being out in the open in such a state is most pleasant. Finally I pull off, crawl onto him, and put my mouth to his. He's most welcoming and, had we not just gained release, I'd swear we were starting up. Finally I ease back and look him in the eye. "Been wanting you for some time," I confess.

"All you had to do was ask." He slips his arms around me, kisses me.

"It's not so easy for a lawman," I explain. "I can't be seen mooning after a man, so it's been hell resisting you."

"I knew it all along," says Ray and when I scoff at this, he insists it's true. "I could feel it on you every time you came near. No matter how lawful your words, your look told another story, but I had the same problem as you. Couldn't really be seen playing up to the marshal."

In the back of my mind this is suspect, but the back of a

man's mind is seldom where he does his thinking. Up front I am downright giddy at him feeling the same as me.

"Wish you could have gotten to me sooner," he adds.

"Well, I have now."

We strip off everything and spend considerable time exploring each other, hours disappearing as we poke, prod and lick. I've never felt such affection and after a good bit we're worked up again. This time I take him on his back so I can see the passion on his face. I take things slow, his legs up on my shoulders, while he works himself to an impressive spew. When I finally pump my last into this man I now know I love, I feel sleep beckon and soon as I pull out, I fall over and give way. And in the morning I wake to find Ray dressed and sitting on that rock, pistol in hand.

My blanket is over me, which is a kindness on Ray's part, having covered me up after he fled our nest. My prick is hard like usual and the irony of such a state is not lost on me. "Maybe you'd best go ahead and shoot," I say. "End whatever in hell this is."

"Don't you know?" he asks.

"Well, I thought I did last night, but now I'm not so sure."

"I won't hang."

"You stick around just to tell me that? A thinking man would be long gone, taking my horse, pistol and maybe even my clothes."

"You keep saying what a thinking man would do. Does that mean I don't think?"

"It means you don't think criminal. Like it or not, your still being here says maybe more than you want."

"Says what?"

"That your heart got loose last night and maybe it carries some weight; that you don't want to let go of what we got started. Running has lost its appeal, which is a good thing, only you're not seeing that because you're scared. I understand that, Ray, truly I do, but I believe I can stand up for you and get justice to work in your favor. You have to trust me on that." Here I draw back the blanket. "The morning's cold. Why don't you get in here and warm up. Then we can talk things over."

There's dew on the ground and we're both without a coat, having come out unplanned. I can see Ray is chilled. "You said I was notable," I remind him. "How about you take advantage of that?"

The gun goes loose in his hand and a sadder sight I've never seen. His shoulders slump with the weight of deciding, and I lay in torment, fear taking hold of me, only it's not fear of getting shot, it's fear of losing him. He holds out a few more minutes, fingering the gun, then finally sets it aside. "Undress," I say and he does. When he gets under the cover with me I kiss him. "I couldn't bear you getting away," I say, "and that's the man talking, not the marshal."

"I'm scared to death, Marshal. You really think you can keep me from hanging?"

"I'm notable for other things, Ray, and the law is one. I'll fight for you and believe I'll win. You'll walk free and we can continue what we've gotten started, such as we can in town."

"Maybe come back here from time to time," he says.

My response is to draw him to me and seal the deal the best way a man can.

DIRTY TOWN

Shane Allison

I was so happy to make it to New York; I could have kissed her concrete. I had only dreamt of it since the sweet age of sixteen. Didn't think I would ever escape the Bible belt of Tallahasseans, with their churches on every corner. "Watch who you drink with," Ma said, as we hugged each other good-bye all teary eyed.

I was nervous but excited. I couldn't wait to get rid of my folks, to venture out into the mouth of madness that was my new home, but there was no rush. My roommate Scott didn't show up until three days later, so the hardwood floors, the stripped mattresses and the view from the top were all mine. I fantasized about my roommates and me fucking in close quarters, doing things to one another that was our secret alone. Scott had finally arrived. As it turned out, he wasn't half bad looking. Quite cut for a nerd.

"When did you get here?" Scott asked.

"A few days ago. My folks drove me up. You?"

"I came by bus. I didn't think I would ever get here with all of the transfers, and the driver kept stopping for bathroom breaks every ten minutes."

"If you think a bus is bad, try drivin' all th' way up from Florida. Ain' nothin' worse than bein' cooped up in a mini van that smells like hot sauce an' barbecue pork skins with a hollin' two-year-old."

"You have me beat," Scott laughed. "What part of Florida?"

"Tallahassee. I figured it was time fo' a changa scenery."

"I thought I sensed a Southern accent."

"So where you from?" I asked.

"Here, New York."

"Manhattan?"

"Queens actually. Far Rockaway. My mother and brother live there. I was teaching in Connecticut before coming back here to get my PhD in economics."

I lied and told Scott that I was a media communications major. It sounded more practical than creative writing. Scott and I didn't wind down for bed until four that morning. The week had taken its pound of flesh out of the both of us with exhausting bus and car rides and the excitement of new digs. That first night Scott wore a wife-beater that showed off his freckled arms. It was the first time I'd slept in close proximity to someone else without sex involved.

Weeks passed. We were well into the semester before our relationship soured. Because of the demands of his classes, Scott was always stressed. He had grown mean, easily annoyed. So I started to avoid him. My classes met only Tuesday and Wednesday evenings. I job-hunted by day and hopped from bar to club most nights while Scott was cooped up with his nose in a book. I'd get home and he'd be asleep at his desk, drooling onto his reading material.

The place was a fucking wreck when I came in from class one night.

"What th' hell is this? Wha'choo doin'?"

Scott never turned around to look at me, but remained motionless at his desk. "Excuse me?"

"You heard me, man. Why all your clothes out in tha floor like this?"

"I was looking for something."

"Yeah, but damn, you ain't have to tare up tha place."

"I'll clean it up."

"No shit you go'n clean this up. What's your problem?"

"I said I'll clean it up!" Scott stormed past me in a rage, out the door. It was scary to see him act a fool like that. It took me the rest of that night to straighten up, to put shit back in order. I looked at the clock sitting on the sill of my window with its devastating view of Ground Zero—you could still smell the ashes. It was a little after four in the morning when he returned and undressed for bed. I watched with squinted eyes as he stripped. He was lean and lithe, his chest peppered with freckles, his shapely butt in boxers. My dick stiffened.

"Wherejoo go?"

"For a walk around the Seaport," he said.

"You okay?"

"Yeah. Sorry about the mess."

"Don't worry 'bout it."

That night we talked until our eyes ached for sleep—mostly about his mom, who was pretty sick, and who doted on his deadbeat brother but treated Scott as if he were invisible.

Scott eventually slept, oblivious to the clatter of battered, smoldering steel being hauled. I lay awake, settling my sleepy eyes on Scott's brawny legs hanging limp off the side of his bunk. I longed to shrimp his perfect, pedicured toes, kiss the soft, pink heels of his feet, worship the arches. I slid my hands down into the warmth of my pajama bottoms imagining Scott's dick between my lips. I studied him as he tossed and turned. I saw a single hand ease its way down into his underwear. I kept pace with him until I came.

That next morning, the sound of the shower woke me. Scott's clothes were lying on his bunk. The dorm room smelled of freshly brewed coffee. There was a note attached to the fridge that read: *Help yourself,* with an arrow pointing to the coffee-maker. It wasn't like him to do something nice. I figured he was apologizing for the mess he'd made of the place.

I poured myself some coffee and while it cooled I sat at my desk to proofread a couple of poems.

As I read my verse, I heard the sudden shutting off of the shower. Steam spirited out into the hallway. Scott came into the room soaked and wet with a beach towel wrapped around his waist. Pearls of water trickled down his legs, and a damp trail of red hair ran from his chest down his belly toward his pubes. He was even cuter without his glasses.

"Hey. Good morning."

"Thanks for tha coffee."

He held the towel tightly around himself with one hand as he fished out a pair of boxers and some socks. What happened next caused my blood to run white hot: an end of Scott's towel dropped, exposing his bare butt and a side view of his dick. I drank in his stark nudity before he pulled the end of the towel back around his ass. My dick twitched and filled as Scott dressed, working his legs into clean boxers, then into starched jeans. I was so busy studying him I burned my mouth on the coffee.

"Are you all right?"

"Yeah. I jus' burned my lip."

"How is it?"

"Pretty good. It's got an interestin' taste. Wherejoo get this from?"

"A café in Chelsea called Big Cup. They have all kinds of blends."

"Cool. I'll check it out."

"You have class tonight?" Scott asked.

"One. You?"

"No. But I was thinking about taking in a movie if I'm back in time. You want to join me?" It was the first time he'd offered to do something with me.

"Sure. Give me a call." I gave him my cell number. "Where you headed?"

"Far Rockaway."

"Is it your mom?"

"She called yesterday. Says she has a doctor's appointment. She's a diabetic on dialysis. She won't go by herself and won't take the train. Not since she got mugged a few years back. And she doesn't trust taxis."

"What about your brotha?"

"Can't find him. I called the number my mom gave me, but all I get is voice mail. Wherever he is, he better stay there because I'm not going to have a brother when I do find him."

"Does he have anything t' do with yestaday?"

"Yeah. Juggling school and dealing with my brother's shit on top of it is taking its toll, you know?"

"Lemme know if there's anything I can do."

"Thanks." He grabbed his pack and headed toward the door.

I spent most of the day thinking about Scott and how he was faring with his mom. I understood his plight. I have uncles with alcohol and heroin addictions and I know how taxing that shit can be on family. Can't help them unless they want to help themselves.

Everyone dug my poems in class that night. High on praise, I strolled through Tompkins Square Park on my way to this bar called Spain where I drank cheap booze and ate stale chicken wings. By the time I left, I only had two bucks to my name. Barely enough for a pack of Ramen. I hoped money from Ma was on the way 'cause I was getting down to saltine crackers and a can of sardines.

After my glimpse of Scott in his birthday suit that morning, I had walked around campus all day with the hard-on from hell. I detoured to the NYU tearooms; they made the food-court toilets and cruising parks back home look like convents, and the men of New York were gorgeous and freaky—unlike the trolls back home. The A-level toilet at Bobst was a smorgasbord of men sucking and receiving. I was happier than a fly on shit that I didn't have another class for the rest of that week. I spent it applying for jobs as movie theater ushers and copy center techs. I would choose ten places a day to apply, and then it was off to the tearooms, where I spent three to five hours scavenging for college boys. Figured if I couldn't be a student there because of shit grades and blue-collar parents, I might as well cruise the bathrooms, sucking West Village dick. I ended up fucking a saucy Blatino boy in a handicapped stall, then rode the A-train back to Fulton with cum on my breath.

Scott hadn't called, and the room was pitch black when I got in and he was dead to the world. His covers were kicked off, and one of his legs was dangling off the side of the bed again. Careful not to wake him, I set my backpack against the closet door. My bladder was bursting with appletinis. After I drained my dick, I went straight to bed.

That night something startled me out of my drunken slumber, and it wasn't the goings-on of steel being hauled. I had grown accustomed, able to adapt to the New York noises.

I looked to Scott asleep in his bunk. Without my glasses, he was but a blur. I grabbed them off the cover of the collected poetry of James Schuyler. Scott was at it again, tugging at his dick. I relaxed back into bed, hand under my cotton tent as I watched. He grunted lustfully across from me. He let loose a breathy sigh when he came. Through squinting eyes, I watched him climb out of his bunk. He unfurled some towels from the kitchen to wipe up his mess. Scott had quite the porno dick for a nerdy boy. Mine throbbed so under my comforter, I could have come without touching it. He discarded the stained paper towels and went back to bed. I turned away from him and tried to think of something other than his jack-off session. That next morning, he said nothing; not a word was uttered about the night before.

"So how did th' trip t' your mom's go yestaday?"

"Not so good. She's actually worse off than I thought. When I got there, the place looked like a landfill. I spent half the day cleaning up. I asked her where Joe was and all she could tell me was that he was working, when I know he hasn't worked a legit job in months other than slinging dope."

Scott made my dick ache as he walked the floor half-naked. All that skin, the alabaster muscles.

"So were you able t' get'er th' medicine she needed?"

"I told her I would take care of her prescriptions from now on."

"It'll work itself out. You jus' gotta take it one day atta time."

"Yeah, I guess. So what do you have planned today?"

"I gotta fin' a job. U'm goin' broke. I thought my financial aid would have come through by now, but nothin'. I checked with them Wednesday and they said it will probably be another three weeks."

"You want me to lend you a couple of bucks to tide you over?"

"No, U'm good."

"C'mon," he said, fishing two twenties out of his wallet. "Here."

"Scott I cain't, man, really."

"I insist."

I took the cash reluctantly. "I'll pay you back as soon as I get some money."

"You seem like you're good for it." He went into the bathroom to shower.

The door was slightly ajar. I stared at the blur of his body through the sheer of the shower curtain, at the curve of his ass, his dick dripping with lather. I wanted to stay, but I needed to go job-hunting—though his dick was the only job I wanted.

I spent the day applying anywhere with a HELP WANTED sign in the window. All I could think about was Scott. So much so, I wrote his name on an application by mistake. By late afternoon, it was time to cruise. The security guard who usually gave me shit wasn't on duty; instead, a fat gospel-singer of a woman with hoop earrings and a weave down to her ass, let me pass into the building.

The bathroom reeked of pee. Most stalls were occupied 'cept for the shitter at the end, the one with the larger glory holes. I glanced in at the cruiser next to me, studied what he was so frantically working between his legs. It was long and cut with a perfect set of balls. He was the dirty-blond punk I had sucked off a week before. I signaled him to stick it through. The belt from his shorts skimmed along the floor. I sucked him hard and steady. My muscles burned in my bent position, but the pain was worth it. The scent of musky crotch hair filled me. Spit trickled down his balls. I imagined that it was Scott. A few men that had been lingering at the urinals sauntered over. They beat off as they watched my actions. He didn't give me much of a warning when he came. Just like a punk. I spat him into the toilet and wiped what was left with the sleeve of my shirt. I finished off a few more including Keerati, a computer aide in one of the labs on campus. My legs felt like rubber. I walked like a crippled old man back up the stairs. When I arrived back at the dorm, my favorite stud muffin of a guard was on duty.

"Wassup?" I asked, searching my pockets for my wallet.

"You cool. You up in Four-B right?"

"Yeah. 'Preciate it."

I was surprised that Scott wasn't home. I put away the groceries I'd bought with the money he lent. I was glad he wasn't there. It gave me a chance to search for evidence that would shed some light on Scott's sexual preference.

I rummaged through desk drawers of stationery and books, checked his closet full of pressed Oxfords, blazers and shoes lined in perfect rows, but nothing. No sign of videos, magazines, gay or straight. Not even so much as a Boy George album tucked away. I made sure I put everything back. Neither a shirt nor argyle sock was out of place.

I had popped a TV dinner in the microwave and gone over a few new poems I wanted to work on for the next workshop when I heard Scott outside the door. I felt like a wife waiting up for her husband to come home from a day hard at work. He was armed with plastic bags that read *Szechuan Tasty House Chinese Restaurant* in red lettering.

"Hey." He sat the food on the kitchen counter.

"Oh, you're already having dinner."

"Yeah, but I always got room for Chinese. Wha'joo bring?" I grabbed some plates from the cabinet.

"I got some Chicken Chow Mien, Moo Goo Gai Pan, Shrimp with Lobster Sauce, and a coupla egg rolls."

"Look like you cleaned 'em out."

"Pretty much."

"Di'ja get any fortune cookies?"

Scott held a few up out of the bag. "What's Chinese food without fortune cookies?"

Wasn't long before the entire apartment smelled of Chinese takeout. Scott and I filled our bellies with everything from Chicken Chow Mein to fried rice.

"Di'joo go see your mom?"

"Yeah, she's doing much better." Scott's mouth was greasy from the food.

"I caught up with my brother, too."

"How's he?"

"Busy killing himself with that shit he's putting in his arm. I gave him some money and told him to stop coming around, that he was only upsetting our mom."

Scott was near tears. He turned his head toward his plate to keep me from witnessing his pain. I flipped the script of the conversation on to the cookies that held our fortunes.

"What does yours say?" Scott asked.

You have friends and you know it. I thought since the evening ended so well, it would be the perfect time to talk to Scott about what happened, but I decided against it. I didn't want to add fuel to the fire of Scott's situation.

That night I kept a close eye on him. Just as I was about to drift off to sleep, I heard that same rustling from the prior night. There he was again. I wanted to touch it, to lay my hands there, but I didn't want to startle him awake. I kept my distance with my hand down in my drawers as I watched him under his snug tent. He pulled his covers over his actions. I went to the bathroom to finish up. I thought of Scott with each stroke, every caress until I came into the toilet water. I cleaned myself up and started for bed. I knew that something had to be said.

The next morning the sound of pots clattering and bacon sizzling woke me. I rubbed the sleep from my eyes and grabbed my glasses off the nightstand.

"Hope you're hungry," Scott said.

"Sure, yeah."

The table was decorated with plates of bacon and eggs, a saucer of toast, juice and coffee. *He knows*, I thought, but he mentioned nothing all through breakfast. But it was now or never.

"That was good. Thank you." Scott cleared the table. "Ain' know you could cook," I said.

"There's a lot you don't know."

"Can we talk fo' a minute?"

"What's up?"

"It's 'bout las' night. I saw you."

"Saw me? Saw me what?"

"Never mine, um…"

"No. Spit it out. Saw me what?"

"Jackin' off."

"What?"

"In your bunk las' night."

"Bullshit."

"Look, man, its cool. We all do that shit."

"I was scratching my balls," he said turning red.

I thought maybe he didn't realize he was jacking off in his sleep.

"You know what? You wish I was jacking off. I see how you look at me, how you stare. And I saw your magazines."

"You been goin' through my shit?" I asked, checking my drawers.

"Just for the record, you would be the last guy I would fuck even if I were a fag." Scott grabbed his things and stormed out the door. I sat there stunned; I couldn't believe that he denied it. I searched the graduate building in hopes of running into him to apologize, but he was M.I.A. I couldn't keep focused because of our fight. I got back to the dorm thinking that I shouldn't have said anything. I ate some of the leftover Chinese, and went to bed. Scott didn't come in until three that morning. I pretended I was asleep.

"Darryl, you awake?" he whispered. I felt his hand on my arm. "You asleep?"

"Wa'sup?"

"It's my brother." Scott started crying.

"What? Wha's wrong?" I sat up in my bunk.

"They found him at some old abandoned apartment with a needle in his arm. He's dead. They want me to come down and ID the body."

"Oh god, man, U'm so sorry."

"What am I going to do? How am I going to tell my mother?"

"You want me t' go wi'choo tomorrow?"

"Would you?"

"Of course. We'll go firs' thing in th' mornin'."

"I'm sorry...about last night," Scott cried.

"Hush. Forget about it. I was an asshole."

Scott reminisced throughout the night about himself and his kid brother, how they fought over everything from Tonka trucks to girls in high school, but always made up after the dust settled.

That next morning, Scott was sullen. I practically had to dress him and push him into the elevator. He didn't talk much on the train to Far Rockaway.

"I can't."

"What?"

"All those terrible things I said. I can't see him."

"You ain' mean none of that stuff. He knew that."

"Telling him to stay away from our mother was the last thing I said to him."

"Don't bea'cha self up. He knew you loved 'im."

When we arrived to the coroner's office, Scott froze at the door.

"You can do this, Scott. I'll be right there wi'choo."

"You've been so cool with me throughout all this," he said.

"That's what friends are for."

We walked up to the administration desk where an older, well-dressed woman sat shuffling papers and folders.

"Excuse me. I'm here to speak with a Detective George Geletka."

"Name?" she asked flippantly.

"Scott Whelks."

"Is he expecting you?"

"He called me yesterday, yes."

"Hold on. I'll page him."

"Thank you."

Scott and I waited in the lobby studying those in white lab coats, others with guns and badges hanging from their waists. A middle-aged man with dark hair, who resembled Edward James Olmos, made his way toward us. His badge hung from a chain that dangled around his neck. I knew it had to be him, the bearer of bad news.

"Mr. Whelks? Hi, I'm Detective Geletka. I believe we spoke on the phone."

"Hi," said Scott.

"I'm sorry that we have to meet under these circumstances. We found your brother after we raided a crack house in Dix McBride Apartments. Because he had priors, we were able to identify him as Joseph Whelks. He had you down as next of kin."

"Can I see him?" Scott asked.

"Sure, but I'm afraid that only family is allowed in."

"He's a friend of mine."

"Well, all right. I guess it'll be fine," said the detective.

I wanted to hold Scott's hand to show him just how supportive I was, but it didn't seem appropriate.

"I must warn you that the...smell can get pretty bad."

He wasn't lying. The stench of death was almost immediate. We noticed one of the examiners hovering over a pale, cold corpse. I had never seen a dead body before. Plenty of dead coons, squirrels and 'possums that had fallen victim to Mack trucks, but nothing that real, that close up and personal.

"This is Doctor Turner, our medical examiner."

"Hi," said Scott.

"He's here to identify his brother. Whelks, Joseph C.," the detective told Dr. Turner.

"Right this way."

Scott looked as if he was together. Dr. Turner peeled the white shroud slowly from the body that lay beneath it. I looked to Scott to catch his reaction as we stared upon the corpse of Scott's kin.

"Is this your brother?" asked the detective.

"That's him. That's Joe."

"I'm terribly sorry," said Dr. Turner. I consoled Scott as he started to weep.

"Thanks, Doc," the detective said.

The three of us stood in the corridor outside the coroner's office. I held Scott in my arms as he sobbed uncontrollably.

"Are you his only relative?"

"Our mother. But she's ill," said Scott.

"There's some paperwork we're going to need you to fill out in order to release the body."

Scott's face was flushed red with tears.

"Detective, can he come back tomorrow for all of that?"

"Whenever's good for him," he said. He looked at us as if he thought we were partners. "Here's my card. If he has any questions, please have him give me call, and again, I'm sorry."

"Thank you."

We got back to the apartment, where I fixed Scott a cup of coffee.

"You want me t' call ya mom?" I asked.

"That's okay. I'll go out there later and tell her. I just can't right now."

"I can go wi'choo."

"She doesn't really take too well to strangers. Are you gonna go to class tonight?"

"I thought I would stay here wi'choo tonight an'…"

"No, you should go. I'll be fine."

"But I wanna stay."

"I'll be okay."

"Well…'mkay."

"Thanks for going with me. It meant a lot."

I was quiet in class, doodling in the margins of my notebook, thinking of Scott. My friend Matt asked if I wanted to go for drinks, but I took a rain check. I wanted to get back home in case Scott was there, which he wasn't. He left a note on my desk: *Gone to Mom's. Will call you later, Scott.*

I decided to take a stroll on the Seaport. I took my cell in case he phoned. It wasn't until I was about to hop in the shower that my cell toned.

"Hey."

"Hey," Scott replied.

"How's your mom?" I asked.

"She took it really hard. I finally got her down to sleep."

"How you holdin' up?"

"About as well as can be expected. I'm going to stay with her for a couple of days. Just to keep an eye on her, make sure she's okay."

"You want me t' talk t' ya professors?"

"No need. They know about Joe and I told them that I needed some time."

"'Mkay, well, if you need anything, jus' gimme a call."

"I will."

I spent the next few days busying myself with writing. The money from Ma as well as the work/study check had finally arrived. I spent some on groceries, more on those books that I wanted but didn't have the dough to buy, and banked the rest. I put the forty dollars I owed Scott in an envelope and placed it on his desk. I didn't go to the sex clubs that night. I wasn't interested in toying with the boys in the basement of the Unicorn. I wanted to be with Scott. I locked myself in for the night. I killed the lights 'cept for the one that glowed brightest next to my bed. I watched the people below until I faded off to sleep. Those few days flew by. Scott returned from Rockaway.

He wasn't the same, but quiet, like he used to be during those early days when he moved into the dorm. He was distant with me, sometimes cold. I could tell he was still carrying around the guilt of his brother's death. When he told me that he was moving back home to take care of his mom, I understood.

"It ain't ya fault ya know."

"What isn't?"

"Your brotha's death. You didn't kill 'im."

"I abandoned him. I turned my back on him when he needed

me. I might as well had have put the needle in his arm myself."

"You need t' face th' fact that ya brotha made th' decision t' do drugs."

"What?" He stopped what he was doing and looked at me with red in his eyes.

"Shut up."

"There was nothin' you could've done."

"Shut your fucking mouth."

Scott grabbed me by the collar and shoved me hard against the closet. Its doors snapped under my weight. All the anger and guilt Scott had bottled up boiled over.

"If only I had stayed."

"And what? Watch 'is every move, be 'is bodyguard? He chose his path." I wanted to drink up his pain, eat his sorrow. "It ain't your fault."

We stood in our dorm, as close as lovers. Scott's lips touched mine. Our kisses were not sloppy or pornographic, but like a soap opera, a movie where the guy gets the girl in the end. We stumbled on my bed, our hands beneath shirts, fingers undoing buttons and clasps, dicks in mouths and assholes until we were both sticky with each other. I wish I could say we lay there like two cuddle sluts under the covers, but by morning, Scott was gone.

I spotted him two weeks later at the Sixty-first Street Cafeteria at the buffet. He looked surprised to see me. We caught up over fried calamari and romaine salad. We were both happy that the semester was finally winding down.

"How's your mom doin'?"

"She's in good spirits, healthy. Saturday was Joe's birthday. We went out and put flowers on his grave."

Our conversation felt awkward at first, like we were on some blind date.

"Are you going home for Christmas?"

"I talked t' my mama las' night an' tol' 'er I was comin' home. She sounded excited. I got mosta my stuff packed."

"Are you gonna stay another semester at William Street?"

"I applied t' move in th' Grove Street apartments. It ain't as nice as William Street, but i's closer to campus."

"Well, in case I don't see you before you leave, here's my new number," he said.

As he scribbled it on a napkin, I wanted to touch that hand. I wanted to reach over our table and give him a kiss to prove that he was missed. We cut our time together short due to hectic schedules. We never spoke of that night.

Scott was reluctant to hug me in public. He smelled sweetly of aftershave. We knew it would be the last we would see of each other. We veered off into opposite directions of the Lower Westside. I cried quietly walking along those dirty streets. New Yorkers looked at me wondering what was the matter. I left a piece of my heart on every block, knowing I would never get over Scott.

FLYBOY

Michael Bracken

Ever since I was old enough to comprehend birds I wanted to join them. By the time I was old enough to enlist in the Air Force ROTC, I had a secret I was under no obligation to share and about which the recruiters couldn't ask, a secret that—until recently—could have grounded my military career faster than broken wings grounded the birds I envied.

Throughout college and on through a year of flight school and six months qualifying in my plane, I was able to keep my secret from my fellow airmen by holding my assignations well away from campus and from the base where I was subsequently stationed. That worked until I met Terry.

A tastefully dressed, slim blond, he worked for a property management company that rented houses to airmen who wanted to live off base. When we met in his office, he tried to steer me into an expensive home in an exclusive neighborhood befitting my rank, and it took some effort to convince him that I wanted a home well away from town, surrounded by plenty of undeveloped land, where my private life wouldn't be subjected to prying eyes.

"Why would a handsome captain like you want to live so far from the action?" he asked as he examined me across the top of his desk, taking in my close-cropped hair, broad shoulders and smartly tailored uniform. I kept my gaze steady, staring directly into Terry's pale-blue eyes until a sly smile tugged at the corners of his mouth. Then he said, "I think I know just the place."

Terry stood and I followed him outside to his SUV, admiring the way his cute ass filled out his slacks. Thirty minutes later he led me through a fully furnished split-level well outside of town, with nary a neighboring house within sight in any direction. The decorations were sparse but tasteful, and it wasn't until we stood in the master bedroom and I saw a trio of framed photographs lining the dresser—all of Terry—that I realized we were in his home.

"Are you planning to move?" I asked. By then we had stepped onto the balcony outside the bedroom and were looking across acres of undeveloped grassland. "Is that why we're here?"

"No," the rental agent said as he put one hand on my arm. "It's because I've been turned on ever since you stepped into my office this morning."

As Terry turned to face me, I was certain we were flying in the same formation. I knew better than to play in the same town where I was stationed, but months had passed since I had been with another man and I'd been flying solo far too long. So I didn't stop Terry when he unbuttoned my jacket, pushed it open and placed his hand on my crotch.

Inside my uniform trousers my cock began to inflate, quickly rising to attention. As he dropped to his knees in front of me, Terry drew down the zipper and threaded my erection out through the fly front of my boxers and uniform trousers. He pushed back the foreskin to reveal the swollen purple head of my cock, and then he wrapped his lips around it.

As he hooked his teeth behind the glans, he wrapped one fist around my cock shaft and pistoned it up and down the entire length. After several strokes I pushed his hand away, wrapped my fingers in Terry's hair and held the back of his head as I pushed my cock halfway into his mouth. I drew back and then pushed forward again and again, pushing a little deeper each time until I knew he could handle the entire length.

I hadn't left base that morning anticipating a hookup and would never have intentionally sought one out so close to where I was stationed, yet I found myself with my cock in Terry's mouth, enjoying the feel of his tongue and his teeth on my tumescent member. And I never would have thought myself capable of having an encounter in so public a place as the balcony of someone's home, yet I hadn't stopped Terry when he'd dropped to his knees before me and I certainly had no intention of stopping him after he'd taken me into his mouth.

I drew back and pushed forward, my pace quickening as orgasm drew near. Before I could stop myself, my sac tightened and I came, firing thick wads of hot spunk against the back of Terry's throat. He swallowed as fast as he could, but not fast enough, and some of my cum dripped down his chin. After my cock ceased spasming, I stepped back, pulled it from his mouth and tucked it away.

Terry wiped his chin with the back of his hand and looked up at me. The metal teeth of my zipper had scratched his nose but he didn't seem to notice. I grabbed his hand, pulled him to his feet and together we stepped inside.

"You do this for all your clients?"

"Only special clients," he said with a smile.

We returned to his office and from there, after assurances

that Terry would continue looking for an appropriate rental home, I returned to my quarters on the base. I wasn't sure how I felt about what had happened at Terry's house but I was kept busy the next few days and I didn't have time to give it much thought.

Later that week Terry found a rental house for me a few miles farther down the road, one with a driveway that looped around the house to the garage in back. For the next few years we kept our developing relationship as much a secret as possible, spending all our time at his home or mine and never being seen together in public unless we were far from the base.

Tuesday, September 20, 2011, changed our relationship forever with the repeal of Don't Ask, Don't Tell. I'd not seen the news that day, so I was surprised when I returned home from the base that evening to find Terry waiting in my living room, wearing his best suit.

"Change clothes," he said. "We have dinner reservations."

After Terry told me what we were celebrating, I changed from fatigues into my dress blues and we drove downtown to an Italian restaurant with valet parking, inflated prices and an impressive wine selection.

We started with wine, toasting our good fortune and the good fortune of so many of my brothers and sisters silently serving in the armed forces.

While waiting for our appetizers to arrive, Terry reached across the table and took my hand. After years of hiding our relationship, my instinct was to pull away, but Terry wouldn't let me. He held on fast.

"We don't have to hide anymore."

I glanced around the restaurant, expecting to be the center of attention, but no one was paying any attention to us. I relaxed, took another sip of wine and stared into Terry's pale-blue eyes much as I had the first time we'd met. I knew exactly what he saw when he looked at me, because I saw the same thing when I looked at him.

Our appetizers came, followed by dinner, a dessert we shared and more than one glass of wine. Perhaps we shouldn't have driven home under the influence of all that wine, but we made it without incident.

As soon as we stepped through the back door, we were all over each other, kissing and groping and stripping off our clothes as we made our way to my bedroom. A trail of abandoned clothing followed us, the last of it landing in a heap next to the bed.

I pulled Terry to me and kissed him hard, my tongue thrust deep into his mouth. When the kiss ended, I spun him around and bent him forward. He braced himself on the bed while I grabbed a half-used tube of lube from the nightstand.

After slathering lube over my tumescent cock, I squeezed a glob into my lover's asscrack. I massaged it into the tight pucker of his asshole until I was able to ease my middle finger into him.

Then I pulled my finger away and pressed my fat cockhead against his sphincter. I grabbed his hips as he slowly opened to me but I was impatient and pushed hard, driving myself deep inside him.

Keeping a tight grip on his hips, I drew back and pressed forward, pumping hard and fast until I couldn't restrain myself. I came, and came hard, driving into him one last time before firing a thick wad of hot spunk deep into Terry's ass.

I held him until my cock finally stopped throbbing and I could pull myself free. Then we collapsed on the bed, and I held him in my arms.

"This is the day we've been waiting for," Terry said.

I kissed him before he could say any more. He was right,

but did I have the courage to follow through on my promise to marry him now that a public revelation of our relationship wouldn't ground me? Terry had willingly played second fiddle to my career, but now he didn't have to.

"Tomorrow," I whispered. "Tomorrow we'll tell everyone."

The next day I spoke to some of my fellow pilots, letting word-of-mouth carry the news to everyone on base who mattered. Some of my fellow airmen claimed they'd known which way I flew but hadn't said anything. Others appeared surprised by the news.

Over the next several weeks a handful of other officers and more than a dozen enlisted personnel also came out. None, however, came out by announcing their impending wedding as I had done.

We didn't rush the wedding, but waited until the following January to tie the knot before our closest friends and family. Then we attended a reception at the Officer's Club, thrown in our honor by like-minded airmen.

As Terry and I walked hand in hand into the club, publicly acknowledging our relationship in a way we could not have less than a year earlier, I felt as if I was soaring.

BUT FOR THE GRACE OF GOD, BABY, THERE GO I

Kevin Killian

Dear Jeremy,

When I was your age I lived in the East Village in a rundown old flat. I even had a girlfriend who lived with me, Jolene Turner. She was an artist, and her attitude toward Mark was a quizzical one. Whenever Jolene bothered to consider Mark McAndrew, she thought of him as cheap. Every time she saw him, he was complaining that he had no money. And she knew he had some. But Mark was a professional sponger.

Mark was nearly seventeen and lived out on Long Island, in a little town called Smithtown, with his mom and dad. "They're not my real parents, though," he always said. As though that made it any less shame-making, any less square. He didn't exactly act ashamed of his situation, but he preferred that you didn't bring it up. Mark still went to high school and was usually only in her face on weekends, sometimes not even then. Some weekends he stayed in his little town turning everyone on and attending school functions. "Such as?" Jolene inquired. "Such as…pep rallies, football games, dances, things no one ever asked *you* to go to." He had any number of girlfriends and sometimes he'd bring one of them into the city. Jolene never had the chance to really warm up to any of these girls because they changed all the time. "He changes girlfriends like, one, two, three," she said to me once.

"That's how it should be," I said lazily. "You get in a rut when you're with the same chick."

"We're not in a rut," she said with spirit.

"Oh no?"

"You think we are?"

I kind of mumbled no.

"Well, what d'you mean then?"

"Nothing."

And she couldn't get any more out of me than that. She didn't want to press the issue. What if I wound up booting her out? Where would she go? It was I who had all the bread. Jolene had her art work and all that, but her painting brought in very little bread. No gallery, no one, seemed interested. It was I who was the breadwinner, I and my three trust funds. If I kicked her out, she didn't know what she'd do or where she'd go. One thing to her advantage was that, so far as she knew, I wasn't interested in any other chick. Another, the one that really held us together, was that without her, no one would do my laundry or cook my meals. But she might be so easily replaced that it scared her.

There was nothing about her that made her inexpendable. She had faced that fact squarely and now it only scared her a little. I was twenty and she was twenty-six. I don't remember how we met now.

Mark and I had known each other for years. My father was Ralph Isham, the writer, and he used to live in a place near

Smithtown and I had actually been sent to school out there for a little while. No more than a few months, Jolene gathered, although Mark and I were very vague about this. Mark was naturally vague about it, since he wanted no reminders from her questioning or from anything else that he still lived in Smithtown, in his parents' house. Though, again, they weren't really his parents, or so he said. Certainly he acted as though they were some breed of servants or people he'd rented.

So whenever Mark came to New York, I was always waiting for him and greeted him warmly. If Mark had been a chick, Jolene would have been jealous, but he wasn't. She knew that from personal experience of the carnal knowledge kind.

One night she'd been lying there in bed with the mosquito netting lying over her. A summer night. In the summer she slept with mosquito netting because the nights were so hot as to preclude blankets or even sheets. Even the thinnest of the tie-dyed linen sheets seemed too thick. Yet to be able to sleep, she had to feel all tucked in, so she used mosquito netting. On this particular night she'd been all but asleep and before she knew what was happening Mark's thing, his penis, was in her hand and hot, even hotter than the summer night. It felt clammy and alive, rather like a bat, a vampire bat.

"Mark...!"

It was too hot to sit up in bed, so she just lay there instead, but she did feel awfully weird. And it was too hot to unclench her hand from around Mark's thing so she just held on to it as though it were a subway strap or rolling pin. Once he saw she was awake, he began whispering to her. He rolled away a few yards of the netting and squeezed into her bed beside her. She didn't know what to say because he was such a familiar face and he was my best friend so she was used to him, yet she had only rarely considered what it would be like to have sex with him. Then she let go of his thing and put her arms around him and thought, with a shiver of grief and guilt, that he was the hottest thing she'd ever felt yet instead of wanting him to roll away she wanted him nearer her; she wanted him to smother her with heat. His head, his hair and his face, however, were relatively cool. It was the rest of his body, below his chin, that was hotter. They wound up kissing. At first, because she'd woken holding his thing she'd thought he was naked but he wasn't, he was wearing an old pair of my pajama pants, white cotton, with old elastic holding them up at the waist, with a vent or flap in front out of which his thing emerged, sometimes hard, sometimes soft, hot throughout. The walls of her bedroom were rose colored, purple colored. She had painted them herself, thinking that their colors would give her the illusion of feeling that she lived inside a delicate coral seashell. But that night, she forgot about that part of it and saw only the resemblance between them and Mark's suffused thing. It too was rose and purple. Jolene was quite interested in it that night and played with it for quite a while. All the time Mark was kissing her on the neck or lips with his cool face.

Afterward she felt or thought that she had not known how, mmm, phallically oriented she was. "If that's the word."

Eventually the two of them fell asleep again and when the morning came, she heard a knock, and the door opened, and I stood there with all my clothes on, even a coat and hat.

Jolene gasped.

But I didn't mind. I only laughed. "We're all even better friends now," I said. I got into bed with them. Mark was still asleep. Jolene lay stiffly between me and Mark and tried to explain. She was wearing a nightgown and Mark still wore the pajama pants, but I wasn't fooled; I had immediately guessed that she and Mark had gotten it on. She tried to say that it wasn't her fault but I put my hand over her mouth, saying, "I don't mind. I think it's super cool. I wondered when something like this would happen, and I think it'll bring all three of us closer together."

"I feel like such a fool," she said. "Also to tell the truth I feel very uncomfortable right now, with both of you in my bed like this."

"You'll get over that feeling."

"Some things you never get over, Danny Isham," she said. Then I asked her a hundred embarrassing questions. To ease her embarrassment I tickled her ribs while asking. All the questions were about Mark McAndrew and what he was like in bed. Waves and waves of shame and of laughter contorted her body. Finally all of our noise woke Mark and he looked awful, just awful. What a mess. Which was funny because normally Mark was a very cute, good-looking kid. But yuck, he had bad breath and everything. I on the other hand looked clean and good enough to eat. My breath was fresh and felt like a breath of fresh air.

"What's happening?" Mark asked fuzzily. A long string of hair was stuck in his mouth, which also, along its creases, was dusted with this horrible sleep-dust or yellow crust.

Jolene rose and climbed over Mark and went into the bathroom to look in the mirror to see if she looked as scuzzy as Mark. But she didn't, she looked like her normal self. Nobody had ever given her any beauty prizes and no one ever would, but at least when she woke up she looked like a normal woman and not like a bat out of hell like Mark had when he woke up. She rinsed out her mouth with salt and water, washed her face.

It was funny when she went back to her bedroom though, because now Mark looked fine. He looked like a different boy than the one she'd climbed over not five minutes earlier. The morning was cool and clear. There was even a breeze blowing through the open window. It looked like it was going to be a

beautiful day and, as it turned out, it was. Except emotionally—
for her. All day she walked around wondering what had gotten
into her and if I, while pretending to be cool, was actually pissed
off at her for going to bed with Mark who was my best friend.
Maybe he was. She herself felt stupid for doing what she had,
and pissed off at Mark for starting the situation in the first place.
The whole setup reminded her of Truffaut's film *Jules and Jim*
which she'd seen at the Thalia. *Jolene Turner, I'm surprised at
you,* she said to herself. *Why did you let Mark come into your
bed? You don't even like him and you're certainly not in love
with him.* She determined that if Mark ever tried to ball her
again she would scream or throw hot water on him or kick him
in the balls. Or something.

Something about the night's heat had betrayed her, she
decided. There had been a pearly shine on Mark's body that
had made her feel, for one hot night, that everything was worth
losing if she could hold on to it.

But that wasn't the real Jolene at all. She knew that. That had
been someone else—at best, a dark side of her personality.

The thing was—or what made her feel guilty was—that she
had been so turned on. I, despite my many winning ways and
funny little tricks in bed she'd learned to like, wasn't really that
good as a lover. *Not like pal Mark,* she thought. *I mean, Danny's
okay but he's not very exciting. Like he always comes so fast like
he's in a race or something.* Her aunt always said some men are
built for speed, some for endurance. There were other things that
disappointed her about me in bed but that was the main one.
And really that wasn't such a problem because most of the time
she just wanted the whole thing over and done with anyhow.
It bored her is what it did. Some people just aren't very highly
sexed and she was one, she thought, supposing further that I
was another. So we were well matched. And when she pored

over it further, she didn't suppose that Mark McAndrew was always so good in bed either. His energy and allure last night probably stemmed from the thrill he was getting by making love to the forbidden, or what might ordinarily have been thought of as the forbidden, his best friend's girlfriend. Luckily for Mark, I was accepting and agreeable. There wasn't, she thought guiltily, a mean bone in my body. Whereas Mark's mean streak ran all through him. On the whole she was glad that Mark didn't live in the apartment and visited only on the weekend and not even, thank god, every weekend, because he was so mean and also so cheap. Oh, Mark was okay but she didn't think she could handle having a roommate who was not only mean but cheap into the bargain. So all in all, she preferred me on the whole, even if she had never been very turned on by me or by my lovemaking or my body or my lazy lackadaisical rich-boy ways.

Despite being opposites in many ways, one thing held Mark and me together. It was something Jolene didn't know about, and funnily enough, neither did Mark or I. The thing was that Mark and I were secretly attracted to each other and were both afraid that we were queers.

I had never been to bed with another man and wouldn't even know what to do once I got there. Mark had been to bed with dozens of men but most of them were strangers, just pickups, and he was scared stiff someone he knew would find out he was a queer. He and I were very awkward with each other and rather frightened of each other's power over himself, but each figured that in time all would work itself out, although who knew in what strange or disappointing direction? We had sex on the mind continually. We wanted to go to bed with each other but neither of us knew how. Mark thought, *If I say anything or try anything or start anything, Danny will be repulsed, he'll drop me, he'll hate me, he'll think I'm a queer and I'm not.*

It's just that I love him so much I want to express my love in a more physical way. I'd like to sit on his face. I thought much the same thing about Mark, except I had an extra burden, or so I thought: my fear of corrupting Mark, who was several years my junior. Also, my desires were less localized than Mark's. I didn't know what I wanted. As I said, I wouldn't know what to do with Mark in bed if I had him there. I'd be nervous, blow the whole thing; I certainly never thought of sitting on anyone's face. The whole thing was beyond me. Sometimes I despaired, thought of killing myself, but then what good would that do? So he and I were in a strange predicament and overcompensated in many ways for our perverse feelings by being rather cavalier and sleeping around a lot.

Of course in New York's East Village there were plenty of real queers you could spot a mile away and when Mark and I went for a walk we'd see them running all over town like they owned the place and we'd say, "Wow, look at those queers." "Someone should clean the place up." "They're sick." "I mean, talk about obvious."

My father was queer too. In midlife he'd turned and divorced my mother and moved in with another man. I thought that it might be inherited or passed down from father to son. I wasn't sure what the story was with lesbians but I imagined it was the same kind of thing—only sexes reversed. So, I didn't like to talk about my father and in fact hadn't spoken to him for years and years: I was ashamed of him.

And I thought, *Well, Mark's father isn't a queer so I guess Mark isn't either. Then again, Mark always says that those aren't his real parents and maybe his real father is queer and so, maybe, he's queer too.*

Mark knew all about my father because my father was a famous poet and involved in the peace movement and you always read about him all the time or saw him on TV. But Mark had different ideas about genetic inheritance. He thought, *Wow, it would be too much of a coincidence if Danny was a queer too because the whole world knows about his father and being a queer isn't inherited, you get it from somewhere else, from out of the air, from out of a particular poisoned patch of air, so Danny can't be one because it would be too much of a coincidence. Lightning doesn't strike the same family tree twice.*

But, although Mark didn't know it, lightning had struck twice, and so years later the two of us still pondered the question: which of our theories was more correct, assuming for the moment that there was an element of the correct in either of them. We each thought our own theory correct, but it was something we could never discuss with each other.

I would never admit it, but many times when I masturbated I was thinking in some dreamy unfocused way about Mark.

Mark never masturbated but what he would do was let somebody jerk him off and at those times he would think of, sometimes screaming into the night and into the stranger's surprised face, fucking me. When Mark said to himself, *It's just that I love him so much I want to express my love in a more physical way,* he wasn't even being honest with himself, because what love he had he'd given away long ago to another man; all he felt for me was a reflex physical passion. And so when being jerked off by his real lover, Mark never screamed out my name for fear of hurting Carey's feelings, but it's true he sometimes thought of me and didn't know whether to laugh or cry or merely come.

The whole setup was a vicious circle and resulted in the two of us playing a lot of games with each other and trying to prove to each other and to ourselves that neither of us was a queer. We still had a lot of fun nevertheless, and we enjoyed each other's company immensely, despite there being many differences between us, and despite the secret tension we each felt in the company of the other.

But that was why, for example, I was so pleased when I found Mark in Jolene's bed even though she was supposed to be my girlfriend. This way I got the chance to, as I put it, check Mark out. Plus to feel, or have the option to feel, very self-righteous about it if I wanted to. And I did—want to. Oh very much so!

That, then, was me all over. Rich kid trying to act poor and punk.

But in a way I couldn't help it.

Anyway, the thing is—what I meant to say is that when Mark and I went for a walk we'd see these real queers running all over town like they owned the place and either Mark or I would say, "There but for the grace of God go I." Saying it one way but in our hearts thinking the same thing in another way. "But for the grace of God, baby, there go I."

This is all a long time ago, Jeremy, but God still works in those mysterious ways and when you come back from your meeting, and you're standing at home, bent at some comfortable angle, leaning on your dresser perhaps, with your pants down at your feet, in front of your full-length mirror, writing down for me every detail of what your ass looks like close up, I know you'll feel His grace too. He's there for everybody the way I'm there for you.

With much warmth,
Daniel

CORYDON 13

Thom Nickels

There are a lot of homosexuals in Boston...

Harvard Square in the late sixties was as good a place to live as Paris or Berkeley. I know, because when I walked out of the Harvard Square subway station from Boston for the first time in September of 1969, I was hit with a barrage of images, the most striking being a professor in a beret riding a bicycle. He was even wearing tiny oval eyeglasses that put me in mind of Jean-Paul Sartre.

I had come to the Boston-Cambridge area to do civilian work as a conscientious objector in lieu of military service. I'd chosen this area because it was similar in some ways to my hometown of Philadelphia, and because it was near the sea. I left Philadelphia without knowing where I was going to live or work, but that quickly changed once I arrived in the city via Greyhound bus. I found a room in a Harvard Square rooming house. Although I signed a year's lease that very day, I still had to find a menial job in a hospital. That would come two days later, when I was hired as an operating room orderly at Tufts-New England Medical Center.

After settling in, I wondered who would become my first Boston friend. I knew it wouldn't be Albert, the Kirkland Street Mormon landlord who had a wife and family. It would also certainly not be the very cosmopolitan Dr. Stein, who gave me my employee physical.

Dr. Stein, with her prominent gray streak, was very familiar with the alternate service that conscientious objectors were required to perform, and told me about several COs currently working at the hospital. Although her words were comforting, she perplexed me when she stated, "There are a lot of homosexuals in Boston."

I didn't tell Dr. Stein that I was homosexual, nor did I say anything that would cause her to think that. I was not effeminate, at least as far as I could tell, so her labeling me as such was a mystery. In an odd way her comment also managed to reassure me that I'd made the right decision in choosing Boston. Sadly, the prescient Dr. Stein, who was fairly advanced in years when she gave me the physical, dropped out of sight once I began my employment, though I looked for her often in the hospital hallways.

My search for a friend had to wait till after my eight-hour shift as well as the two hours I spent writing every night.

It was the writing that led me down my first false path. While I was in the rooming house's communal kitchen one night, a handsome Serbian student, Mark, asked me, "Who does all that typing?" Mark lived in a room not close to mine by any means, so it was hard for me to comprehend how the noise from my typewriter could travel such a distance.

"That's me," I confessed, happy that I could finally say that

I was a writer besides being a CO hospital worker. I told Mark that I was trying to write a book, even as the thought occurred to me: Was Mark one of Dr. Stein's homosexuals? Mark was in grad school part-time but worked during the week and was often dressed in a shirt and tie. He had a lithe, appealing body but he generally offered no hints as to his sexuality despite his elfin manner. One night he mentioned that his big passion in life was collecting icons. In time he would suggest that sometime I should come to his room and have a look at them, but since the invitation was halfhearted, the visit never happened.

One evening, feeling lonely, I visited the communal kitchen in the sister rooming house, Manor II, just across the driveway. That's where I met Edwin, a handsome artist enrolled in art school. Edwin told me that he'd come to the Boston area from Wisconsin. I discovered that we had read many of the same books. It also intrigued me that we were both quiet types. *He must be one of Dr. Stein's people,* I said to myself. With this in mind, I was already creating a fantasy of a great writer-artist association along the lines of Isherwood and Bachardy and Auden and Kallman....

"I'd like to see your etchings," I told him. Today that cliché is a joke, but for me at that time it was heartfelt. Most artists like to show their work. But when an invitation was not forthcoming, I wondered if I'd gone too far in my mention of the relationship between Arthur Rimbaud and Paul Verlaine, or had dropped too many hints concerning the bond between Allen Ginsberg and Peter Orlovsky. I'd also been laying it on thick about artists and writers being iconoclasts and experiencing "the new—and the raw..." But this was Harvard Square, after all, not cheesy Wisconsin, where he said he was from.

"We can hang out in the kitchen," he said, seeming to read my mind with uncanny accuracy. At point that our conversation was over anyway because our privacy was interrupted by the entrance of other students, although I managed to get him to tell me his room number. This came in handy the next day, when I wrote him a note and slid it under his door. The note simply said, *Corydon 13*. *Corydon,* of course, was the title of Andre Gide's defense of homosexuality, and 13 was my room number in Manor House I. I liked the idea of a cryptic puzzle; the name Corydon seemed a good choice because the art student had told me that he was also a fan of French literature. He also made it known to me that he was friends with Deena, who lived in my house.

Deena was a charming woman from a wealthy New Jersey family, a Harvard French studies scholar and PhD candidate in her late twenties. She did her red hair up in a Victorian swirl, a cross between Agnes Repplier and Edith Wharton. She could recite Baudelaire in French as well as whole sections from Proust. When I first met her she wanted to know how a nonacademic like me knew so much about French literature. She then asked if I spoke French or had ever traveled to Paris. When I said no to both questions, she seemed deeply puzzled although I confessed that I was led to French literature through the work of Henry Miller and Sartre, and that I had read all of Camus in high school.

"I love French literature, especially the work of Gide, and his scandalous autobiography, *If It Die,*" I told her. She told me that she loved Gide. In the coming months, Deena would invite me to her room for tea. She liked the fact that I was a conscientious objector doing alternate service, and on more than one occasion she asked to hear the story of my leaving home and coming to the Square. She refrained from asking about my private life. In fact, she would not know that I was gay until some time later when she left Manor I for a real apartment house in another part of the Square. At that time, when I went to visit her in her new digs, I told her that I was gay—a logical extension of all our Gide talk—but the news hit her hard. Facing me on the sofa, she blinked and didn't answer for a moment.

"Like Gide," I said, "I am a homosexual."

She continued to look at me as her eyes slowly filled with tears. The fact that she was crying was shocking to me. Did she see me as a pathetic young man who would never be happy? The romance and adventure of Gide's life suddenly went up in smoke: another Deena seemed to be emerging.

"A lot of writers were gay: Proust, Rimbaud, Verlaine, Genet," I countered, reacting to her tears and hoping that a literary approach would get her out of this salty soup and into Dr. Stein's world. But Deena, I am afraid, was feeling something beyond the pale of literature. When I stood up to leave, she gave me a heartfelt hug, her eyes filling up again as she walked me to the elevator.

When Edwin read my note, he took it to Deena and asked for her help in deciphering it. Why he just didn't throw the note away is a mystery, but somehow he tapped into the word Corydon as having a French literature link, and figured that because Deena was the French expert, she would know. She did know, in fact, and told him right away that Corydon was a book authored by Gide and that 13 was possibly a room number. Since there was no room 13 in Manor II, it had to be Manor I.

Edwin knocked on my door sometime in the early evening hours. When I saw that it was him I told him to come in and take a seat. He held the note in his right hand; it was exactly as I had written it, with Corydon spelled out in block letters and the number 13 circled like a symbol from an Aleister Crowley manuscript. I was very excited to see him and flashed him a winning smile but he was as dour as a New England winter.

"Did you write this?" He held the note up to my face like the remnants of a mortal sin or a dirty plate I'd left under his door.

I didn't say anything at first, but there was no way I could stay silent. The idea, of course, was for him to respond to the note but only if he was feeling sexy, not in this corrective way which put me on the defensive. I felt what was coming.

"Yes, I put that under your door. Is anything wrong?"

"The thing is cryptic. I didn't know what it meant but Deena said *Corydon* was a book and that 13 is probably a room so it had to be your room number. Can you tell me what this means?"

"You've never heard of *Corydon*? She didn't tell you?"

"She only said it was a book by Andre Gide…"

"Would you like to sit down?" I offered him a place on my bed but before he could refuse, I pulled out the desk chair and let him sit on that. I explained to him that *Corydon* was Gide's defense of homosexuality based on the early Greek models of Plato and Socrates. He was a good listener and for a while I thought I was getting somewhere, especially when I mentioned Alexander the Great and then did a time lapse to include the relationship between Rimbaud and Verlaine. He continued to listen with a detached interest but it soon became obvious that I wasn't making any headway at all. I stopped myself from telling him that it was not necessary to fall in love or French kiss in order to have *an experience.*

"I am not a homosexual, so why would this interest me? Your note suggests that I'm homosexual. Are you a homosexual?"

I told him that I did not think that he was really homosexual. He had a hard time understanding this. "I know you're not homosexual," I repeated. "I wanted to send you a signal. There are heterosexuals who do not follow party lines. They cross-pollinate. "

The tortured look on his face expanded into a full-brow sweat. He was not a patient etherized upon a table but a constipated guy sitting on the john. "Look, if it offended you, I'm sorry, but I thought as an artist, you being an artist, you'd be interested in expanding your consciousness. The poet Rimbaud says that an artist should experience *everything, everything* as in pushing outside the circle. I thought you were that kind of artist."

"I am an artist but I like women."

I told him that the poet Verlaine liked women as well but that this fact did not steer him away from Rimbaud. I also reminded him that only a few days ago he told me that he did not have a girlfriend. "If you like women but don't have a woman, where is that getting you?" I wanted to say the last part, but held back. The fact is, I didn't want to say anything too outrageous because I knew it would get back to Deena.

Our parting was civil, although after shaking his hand and seeing him to the door, it would be the last time I'd ever speak to him. Throughout that first year in Cambridge I would some-times see him in the predawn hours on my way to the MBTA. He'd be walking in the opposite direction en route from his all night job, while I was on my way to Tufts. We never said hello to each other or even glanced each other's way, not even during one of New England's biggest blizzards when we both struggled to walk through walls of early morning snow drifts. We were the only ones on the street at that hour, and not saying anything struck me as sad. His coming to Harvard Square from Wisconsin to work as an artist, as well as working all night to support himself, didn't seem too different from my own story.

For me, however, the big question became: Where the hell were Dr. Stein's homosexuals?

Homosexuals were everywhere, of course, but the trouble was finding them. I did a lot of walking around Boston on weekend nights trying to spot one. I figured I would know once I happened upon an effeminate man, a so-called queen, who would then lead me to a popular watering hole or outdoor cruising area. I had read about these cruising areas in the novels of John Rechy, and so knew that they were often near public parks. I headed for the Boston Common and the Public Gardens where I watched and waited and walked in circles.

I spotted my first homosexual near the Public Gardens. It was a foggy night, one of those New England autumn evenings full of fresh breezes from the bay. The park area was nearly deserted, but there he was, a tall blond guy in a cape. The cape took me by surprise. I'd never seen anyone wear a cape in Philadelphia, but here was a definite throwback to the nineteenth century, only it was not worn by a paunchy Victorian gentleman with sideburns but by an attractive man who had just left an exclusive social event like an opera.

My heart skipped a beat when I remembered stories of the Boston Strangler, very much in the news just a few years before my coming here. This was gothic glamour at its height: I was being led to the homosexuals by a figure out of *Dracula*.

I knew he was homosexual because of his flaming blond hair, so I followed him at a distance for what seemed like a long time until he led me to a city block where I saw young men standing or sitting in front of a row of townhouses. Then he seemed to disappear, as if he'd been a spirit guide sent to show me *the place*, though I later looked for him among the lineup of young, masculine men in leather jackets and tight-fitting white trousers.

I hadn't made it halfway around the block before a car pulled up beside me. I watched as the driver leaned across the passenger side and asked, "How much are you?"

"What do you mean?" I said, the truth dawning on me as soon as the words left my mouth.

"Everyone's either buying or selling. You're on the wrong block," he said, speeding off.

I knew this wasn't what Dr. Stein had in mind. I called it a night but the following weekend, I left Manor I after dinner and took the MBTA to Washington Street where I resolved to follow through with my plan: go to the adult theater district and ask an adult bookstore clerk where the nearest gay bar was. Adult theater people are used to every variety of sex and would not be shocked or angered by the question, whereas someone on the street might see it as you thinking they were homosexual. Boston's Combat Zone in 1969 was a raw slice of neon with loud honky-tonk bars, large porno-movie palaces and many adult peep shows. The Zone was always crowded with revelers, sailors, obvious prostitutes and rowdy groups of barhoppers. There were strip bars with long presentation runways where topless women in cheap chiffon gowns would strut back and forth among cheering patrons. This was a far cry from sedate Philadelphia, with its much smaller (and tamer) porno district.

The peep-show clerk directed me to the Punch Bowl, and so I found myself, ironically, in the vicinity of the bus station where I had arrived from Philadelphia only a few weeks earlier. Scully Square was less honky-tonk than the Zone but the ground there had a 42nd Street vibration. On the way to the Punch Bowl I spotted a guy about my age in men's casual clothing but wearing a long-haired woman's wig styled like one of the Andrews Sisters. I knew he had to be headed to the Bowl.

At the Bowl I bought a beer and went downstairs to inspect the room that was sometimes used as a dance floor, then walked upstairs where I took in the clientele, many of them stereotypical types I'd read so much about, especially in *Life* magazine: the soft, womanly voices, the feminine mannerisms, not to mention their heavy use of cologne. Among the queens there were many quiet masculine types in V-neck sweaters and tight white Levi's, and a few men in black leather jackets.

A woman with a change pouch went around taking orders and then came back and delivered the drinks. I was on my second beer, thinking this must be the place Dr. Stein had in mind, when a man in an opera cape came up to me.

"My name is Pierre Paul," he said in a thick French accent. He was a little older than me, but not much, somewhat good looking with a slender body and well-defined facial features. The cape put me in mind of the caped stranger I'd followed by the Public Gardens. At this point I was thinking that capes were an important part of the Boston mystique. I introduced myself, and Pierre toasted me with his beer. Because he did not hear a Boston accent, he asked where I was from.

"Philadelphia," I said. "I've been in Boston one month." I told Pierre about my alternative service assignment at Tufts and he told me about his transfer to Harvard from a university in Paris to do graduate work in philosophy. The French connection worked its magic—here was my Corydon 13 at last! I couldn't get the names Rimbaud, Verlaine and Gide out fast enough, confessing to him my love for all things French and even telling him that I was working on a "Gide-like" autobiography. After twenty minutes of conversation, he asked me if I wanted to catch a cab with him back to his place in Harvard Square. "We can ride together and go to my place," he said.

The prospect of riding in a cab with a caped Frenchman was a thrilling start to my two years of alternate service. Once out on the curb, however, he took me aside before hailing a cab.

"Look," he said, dropping the accent, "I am not from France. I am American. I'm from Stamford, Connecticut and I am a Harvard law student. I live in the dorms. I'm sorry for misleading you…it's just that one has to be careful when going to these kinds of places."

"Oh…you're not from Paris at all?"

"That's what I am saying." He smiled nervously as a cab pulled up alongside us and he asked if I still wanted to go back with him. I said yes though I did not tell him how disappointed I was. I was not going to have an affair with a Frenchman after all, but with an ordinary American, although the location of his dorm gave me hope. It was just a few blocks from the Manor, which meant that we could see one another easily and often. The duplicity made me consider the cape's second purpose: would it protect him in a police raid? If the police had raided the Punch Bowl, could he say—in his heavy bogus accent—that he was from Paris and didn't realize he was in a bar of this type? The blond near the Public Gardens might also tell police that he was coming from a classical music concert and was not cruising or loitering like those mannequin boys selling their bodies.

In the cab I felt glad that I'd found my first homosexual, and that experiences such as I had had with Edwin could now be relegated to the past.

"You cannot spend the night," Pierre Paul, who was now Richard, told me.

"My roommate will show up in the morning…."

"Hey Reds, how's it going?"

Greetings like this came from some of the early morning workers waiting for buses or rides along Washington Street. My daily trek to Tufts took me through the Combat Zone in the predawn hours, where I'd often stop at the Hayes Bickford cafeteria for a poached egg. I was never quite sure why these rough worker types said hello. While I always hated the name Reds—to me it had a baseball connotation—I often wondered what these same workers would have thought if they had known that I was a pacifist and a homosexual. For them, seeing me everyday going to work must have put them in mind of themselves when they were young. I'd answer "Fine," or smile, although the greetings never went beyond, "Hey Reds!"

My boss at Tufts, Miss Dowling, was a short woman with red hair and a series of pronounced lines on her forehead, no doubt the result of too many summers without sunblock on the Massachusetts coast. Miss Dowling was constantly giving orderlies, nurses' aides and scrub nurses random orders and reprimands. She impressed me as a workaholic with boundless energy who expected those under her charge to have a similar work ethic.

"This is an operating-room theater," she told me the day I was hired. "We deal with life and death issues on a daily basis. Your job is crucial. If you foul up, that goes up the chain of command. The operations are on a strict schedule. We cannot keep the surgeons waiting. It's imperative that you stop whatever you're doing and go for a patient when you are told to. Wear your lab coat when you leave the theater."

One didn't small talk with Miss Dowling; there were no casual asides about how your weekend went, no questions about issues unrelated to the OR. I was also never allowed to address her by her first name, Dorothy, although a few of the scrub nurses used Dorothy, even Dotty, with abandon. Nurse Shelley, a very feminine Barbie-doll type, was Miss Dowling's favorite. The two of them could often be seen in private huddles. Nurse Shelley called me Thomas and spoke to me as if I was a child. Her condescending attitude had everything to do with an orderly being at the bottom of the hospital totem pole. Like Miss Dowling, she never exchanged pleasantries with subordinates. In fact, during the two years that I worked in the OR, Nurse Shelley would just issue me an order and walk away. It didn't take me long to figure out that she probably had a beef about the CO thing.

Nurse Shelley was popular among the surgeons because of her inability to walk without a wiggle. Her walk, in fact, kept the eyes of many surgeons glued to her bottom when they were not throwing forceps or surgical scissors across the room at an unsuspecting scrub nurse who wasn't keeping up. Nurse Shelley knew how to coddle the egos of surgeons. In many instances she was called into an OR room to replace a scrub nurse who could no longer take a surgeon's abuse.

"Nurse Shelley in Room 6, Nurse Shelley in Room 6," Miss Dowling would announce on the OR intercom.

Surgeon temper tantrums were a common occurrence, erupting at the slightest provocation. A tenuous synergy existed between scrubs and surgeons. One moment there'd be jokes, flirtatious asides and laughter, but then came the sudden downturn. A temperamental surgeon could erupt at the slightest scrub mistake.

Spinal anesthesia necessitated that an orderly hold a patient tight so that the anesthesiologist could inject fluid from a syringe into the patient's back. These procedures were rarely painless and took some time. Often it was the fault of the anesthesiologist if a good hit could not be mastered, although in some cases the problem had no known cause.

I developed a reputation for being able to calm the most nervous patients. My coworker, Will, wasn't as good, but he could clean and remake an OR table faster than I could. Will was African American, my age, and lived in a room in Roxbury not far from his parents' place. He shared a slightly different shift, eight to four, and began work after I opened the OR and had set up all the IV stands in the curtained-off anesthesia area. He would usually arrive in time to help me get the 8:00 a.m. cases from the upper floors.

"Anyone ever tell you that you look like Howdy Doody?" he said to me one day, collapsing over a stretcher in fits of laughter. The Howdy Doody comparison would last two and a half years, the entire time I was at Tufts, and it never failed to send Will into peels of laughter. Sometimes he'd point at me and repeat "Howdy Doody" over and over again, his laughter raging like a fever. Will had a talent for making me see the humor in situations. Sometimes just watching him laugh lightened my mood when the going got rough. I didn't mind the Howdy Doody jokes so much because I was able to see myself through his eyes: a white guy with red hair and freckles. To an African American from Roxbury probably every white guy with red hair and freckles looked like Howdy Doody.

"I'm not taking this anymore, Popeye," I'd tell him. A little later on, when we really began to feel comfortable with one another, I'd call him Buckwheat, referring to the character from the old *Our Gang* comedies. Will would just laugh as much as he did when he called me Howdy Doody. We genuinely liked each other and worked well together as a team, even when Will aimed his barbs at homosexuals. The topic of homosexuality came up thanks to the presence of two flamboyant gay men who worked as orderlies on the upper floors, the most notorious being Wray Wray, a tall muscular African American guy with an Afro the size of Angela Davis's. Wray Wray wore a blue uniform and often assisted me when I had to transport patients to the OR from his floor. I got to know him slowly, although the first time we met the obvious disconnect between his tall muscularity and his petite lady's voice hit me hard.

Here, obviously, was one of Dr. Stein's homosexuals. It was also a sure bet that Dr. Stein had given Wray Wray his preemployment physical exam, something that no doubt led her to tell him what she had told me: "There are a lot of homosexuals in Boston." No doubt she said this to a lot of men she thought might be homosexual. While watching Wray Wray interact with various nurses and physicians, I was always trying to detect hints of disapproval. I found quite the opposite: an acceptance level so relaxed it made me feel embarrassed that I was thinking so negatively. This was Boston, after all.

Will mimicked Wray Wray with gestures like putting his hands on his hips and pitching up his voice. Sometimes he would walk like Wray Wray around the movable laundry cart that we had to bring in from Central Supply twice a day. It was obvious that Will thought that all homosexuals behaved this way, even though I would tell him that I'd met some masculine homosexuals in Harvard Square (a lie), men who could lift a wheel barrel of bricks or throw people Will's size across a room. Will, to his credit, never let a conversation about homosexuals become too serious. They stayed safely put on the comedic Wray Wray level or they gravitated to another Tufts homo-sexual floor orderly, Oswald, a thin white man with almost no personality who was later fired for fellating a patient after giving him a pre-op pubic prep.

"Homosexuals should be killed," Will would say, exploding with laughter. "They are in my neighborhood and they get popped…they walk the street like Wray Wray and pop pop…you see them go down, pop pop… Oh, it's so funny. Oh…oh…"

I did my best to instruct him: You shouldn't think that way. It's discrimination. What would Martin Luther King, Jr. say? Will would never answer me but just refer to something Wray Wray did, and laugh.

During operations, once the patient was asleep, surgeons and scrubs would slip into banter mode: on a good day there'd be lots of sarcasm and joking, even outright flirting. The telling of jokes was common as were stories about friends and families.

In some cases, the jokes would turn to off-color comments or innuendos. Working on hundreds, even thousands of what T.S. Eliot referred to as *patients etherized upon a table,* had no doubt produced this edgy form of humor.

One time a very elderly woman was brought in for an obstruction in her lower abdominal region. She appeared to me as a quiet church lady type. While the nature of the abdominal obstruction had not been noted on Miss Dowling's Patient List, when the woman's X-rays were posted in the OR room the truth of the blockage became apparent: a salt shaker–like object tilting slightly to the side appeared to float in space. The old woman, who had apparently lost the instrument while trying to masturbate, was now the brunt of OR jokes, as long lines of surgeons and scrubs came into the room to take a peek at the X-ray. The poor woman, asleep on the table, had no idea that her case had provided the entertainment for the day.

I was introduced to Padre Basco, an OR technician in his late forties. Basco was of Mexican heritage and had the face of an ascetic. On my first day of work, Miss Dowling assigned Basco to show me how the lockers worked. From that moment on we became great friends. Basco not only had great insight into people, he was great at explaining the bizarre behaviors of the surgeons and scrubs. Later he'd tell me stories about the surgeons, especially how one married Jewish surgeon would haunt the Washington Street porno theaters one night a week looking for gay sex. Basco was popular among the staff, as many scrubs liked to confide in him. Not only had he known great suffering, he'd seen much of the dark side of life but had emerged as a kind of medicine man with a quick wit and an engaging, easygoing style.

"I hate sex," he told me once. "I hate sex because of what

it can do. I hate sex because of what it did to me. I hate sex because for me it became an obsession. I hate sex because it is still an obsession. And it usually has nothing to do with love."

Prior to his employment at Tufts, he'd been an Anglican priest until he was arrested for soliciting an undercover cop. Forced to leave his parish and the priesthood, he decided to move to Boston. Eventually he took up with a poet. They lived together, first as lovers, then as platonic friends in an apartment on Commonwealth Avenue. A small collection of his partner's poetry was published by Basco after the poet's death. In that collection, *Johannine Appendage*, the poet writes that...

Death is grabbing everyone
The learned and the unlikely ones
Into that pavilion
Sumptuous beyond belief
The busier apes and the silent ones
On that miraculous non-journey to a tepid sea.
Stones, knocked down before the setting sun
Death is grabbing everyone
Hagios Ho Theos...*everyone*

It confused me when Basco told me that his relationship with his poet friend was platonic despite their twenty years together. I was not yet aware that sexual passion didn't last forever although I had read a great deal about how homosexual relationships don't last in pre-1969 *LIFE* magazine and *Newsweek* articles. When I'd question Basco about his relationship with the poet, he'd tell me that when it came to sex he found it "elsewhere." A few years later I'd come to know what that "outside" meant when he took me on a guided tour of Boston's sexual underworld, the massive labyrinthine old movie houses on Washington Street in the city's Combat Zone, where the married Jewish doctor went.

Hearing Basco talk about how he and his poet friend were only united in "spirit" made me wonder if I'd ever find a lasting love. It frightened me to think that passionate attachments over time devolve into primarily emotional connections where sex is left behind or becomes sterile and perfunctory. Basco had even told me that a long-term monogamous relationship between two men was impossible because at some point the men have to make peace with "the occasional other." In a way I was facing the unpleasant fact that maybe Basco was proof that older homosexuals have a hard time acquiring long-term lovers and that by necessity they are either forced to live lives of celibacy or they must seek out places like Washington Street.

I told Basco about Pierre, the bogus Frenchman.

"He lied to me... He was wearing a cape the night I met him in the Punch Bowl. This was the same night I saw another gay man in a cape circling the Public Gardens. He had me convinced. The accent was perfect. I thought he was from Paris."

"Oh no," Basco said, laughing that laugh of his that suggested that I'd met a recognizable type he knew all too well. "Don't go giving your heart away to bogus art," he added, accenting the word bogus as if it was a dart thrown across the room.

I told Basco that Pierre would write me letters and make plans to come visit, while insisting that he could not be seen entering or leaving my place and that I should never, under any circumstances, take it upon myself to walk to his dorm for an impromptu visit.

"As if I would actually do that; he's so paranoid, thinking I would walk over to his place out of the blue," I said, one eye out for Miss Dowling, who respected my friendship with Basco but who didn't like to see me talking to him for too long. "Once he wrote me a note on fine stationery commenting on my typewriter and 'the writer's desk,' but we don't really talk. He won't go out to dinner or have a drink with me because he thinks that risks exposing him to classmates. When he comes to my place, he leaves right after we make love. I'm surprised he doesn't wear the cape."

During one of Pierre's visits to the Manor I discovered that he had an artificial right ear. I hadn't noticed it before, but one evening while we were making love I went to kiss it and felt a hard substance much like plastic. Pierre had hoped to interrupt my ear kiss with a quick, "Don't do that," but it was too late. My tongue had already unlocked the secret.

"I should have told you," he said, turning his head to the side. "When I was a teenager I lost it in an automobile accident."

I was not disgusted because my hospital work had made me immune and blind to many physical glitches. I even surmised that he was probably a nicer person as a result of his artificial ear.

"It looks very real," I said. "You would only know the truth if you touched it." I did not want to interrupt our lovemaking so I delayed asking questions, although a kind of newspaper banner headline crossed my mind: *What else about this guy is false?* I couldn't help but imagine the rush of pain he must have experienced the moment his ear was hacked off. Images of his ear flying across the street and making a U-turn to him before landing in his shirt pocket, or even landing by a fire hydrant, flashed through my mind. Pierre, in true opera cape style, was much too discreet to give me details although he did indicate that there had been great pain.

"After great pain, a formal feeling comes," as Emily Dickinson wrote.

Basco said that the story reminded him of Luke chapter 22 where Peter steals a sword from a Roman guard in the Garden of Gethsemane the morning Jesus was taken away, and slices off the ear of Malchus, servant of the high priest, after which Jesus tells Peter to stop and goes up to the servant and holds his head tight until the ear is mysteriously reattached.

Like the surrogate father he would become, Basco told me not to put too much energy into Pierre. I had already accepted the fact that Pierre was beginning to withdraw from me because he felt a long-term involvement would compromise his future. Pierre would later tell me that he did not want to be homosexual at all because homosexual love was impossible, and that it was his plan to marry and have children so that he could pursue a career in law, which I imagine included a judgeship of some sort. My days with Pierre were numbered, so I knew I'd soon be back at square one, which meant that I had to return to the Punch Bowl and meet somebody else. I was still piqued that Edwin from Manor II wouldn't talk to me. "There's no reason for you to give up. You just started," Basco said. "Boston is full of men."

I told him that Dr. Stein had said practically the same thing during my employee physical, after which Basco gave me a knowing smile because he, too, had been examined by Dr. Stein years ago, although he did not say that she had told him that Boston was full of homosexuals.

When Pierre stopped coming around, I returned to the Punch Bowl in search of another love. In those years, I had no idea that the Punch Bowl was an iconic place, and that celebrities like Robert Mitchum and Rudolf Nureyev were occasional visitors. I went back, hoping to repeat the magical night in which I met the "Frenchman," but nothing happened, so I was reduced to hitchhiking into Cambridge because I had missed the last MBTA across the Charles. I had gotten a lot of practice hitchhiking in Pennsylvania prior to my taking the Greyhound to

Boston. Hitchhiking was the norm in 1969, although thumbing it on a highway at two in the morning was a first for me. I figured I might get lucky and meet someone coming home from the bars.

I stood near the Charles River Bridge parallel to the closed MBTA and watched as a car pulled up beside me. I could see that the driver was a single male in a checkered hunter's jacket. He was a short, stocky guy with a round slightly pockmarked face that was not entirely unattractive. Immediately after I told him where I was going he asked me if I wanted sex. His bluntness caught me off guard, but I was so lonely I said we could head to my place. Charlie lived with his parents in Dorchester and worked as a milk deliveryman. When we got the sex over with, he asked me if we could do something the following weekend, promising to take me to the Other Side, a bar with live bands and dancing. I felt sad that it wasn't Pierre asking me out, but I said yes.

When I told Basco about Charlie I said that he looked like Dopey in *Snow White and the Seven Dwarfs,* and that he didn't have much personality. About this time, I heard from an ex–college professor in Baltimore—where I went to school before dropping out to become a CO—that Judy Garland was hanging out in Boston's Napoleon Club, a posh bar for older gay men in the vicinity of the Punch Bowl. I had heard Punch Bowl men refer to the Napoleon Club as a "piss-elegant wrinkle room." The place had a piano, and a chandelier of sorts, and it was said to be structured like a townhouse. Since I wasn't seeing Charlie until Saturday, I decided to find Napoleon's and look for Judy Garland on Friday.

This was a year before Stonewall, a time when Judy Garland was at the height of an end-stage drinking problem. For years I'd heard my mother talk about Judy Garland's drinking problem, and now here was my ex–English professor telling me I needed to find her before she drank herself to death.

When Friday came, I dressed up because I had heard that men were required to wear jackets at Napoleon's. I didn't wear a tie because I knew that more likely than not, I'd be stopping in at the Punch Bowl before heading home, and maybe even hitching a ride home again. The club was hard to find but when I finally walked through the doors I had the feeling that it was not a bar at all but an elegant supper club. It had the look of a Victorian French restaurant: there were elaborately framed oil paintings, Oriental rugs, that chandelier and random high-backed chairs placed beside display tables. Several men were seated at the first-floor bar, all of them in suits. I did a fast walk-through to see if the place merited a longer stay, looking for a slumped-over singer either at the piano or on a bar stool surrounded by men. When I didn't see Judy on the first floor, I headed up the club's narrow staircase, which was much like the staircase in a private home, and surveyed the second bar, just as elegant as the first. My heart skipped a beat when I saw a woman in the corner of the room surrounded by fawning men but a second glance revealed that she was no Judy. The legend was nowhere in sight.

Maybe she's already drank herself to death, I thought.

I left the bar. I didn't know where I was going. I didn't want to go to the Punch Bowl again, so I explored the streets after stopping by the Greyhound bus station as if to recall the morning of my arrival. By accident I came upon the Other Side. Not only was the club bigger than the Punch Bowl, but it had a bluish façade that promised a different kind of experience. Inside, I could see that it was arranged like a nightclub with small café tables positioned in front of a large dance floor or stage. The dance floor was crowded with men fast-dancing to the songs of the day. Once again, Dr. Stein's prediction hit pay dirt.

Outside, I noticed another bar across the way, Jacques, and decided to have a beer there, because you never know where a drunken Judy Garland might wind up. I stayed there until closing time, when a lithe Joan Baez–type approached and asked if she could crash at my place for the night. Her directness caught me off guard. I was in the market for a boy, not a girl, yet here was a girl in need, and since I had nothing but Dopey, a girl might be better than a dwarf. Besides, she looked sort of like a boy with her slender frame and long, straight brown hair.

I told her I lived in Harvard Square, and she said that was fine, she'd pay for a cab, and so off we went. Back at the Manor, I had no idea where this was going, especially since I had a twin bed that could barely hold one person let alone two. The arrangement forced us to cuddle in a spoon position, with our clothes on, although I remember thinking at the time that I would have gladly removed my clothes had she made the first move, but because she did not, I remained dressed but with my arms around her. When morning came, I told her to stay put while I went out and bought orange juice and muffins. After we ate, she thanked me and we said good-bye.

I never saw her again, but I did see, for the very first time ever, Julia Child shopping in the local Kirkland Street market, looking over some heads of lettuce.

ABOUT THE AUTHORS

SHANE ALLISON has had poems and stories published in *Best Gay Erotica, Ultimate Gay Erotica, Best Black Gay Erotica, Best Gay Love Stories, West Wind Review, Fence, Between: New Gay Poetry,* and is the editor of many anthologies for Cleis Press including the best-selling, Gaybie-award winning *College Boys,* and *Hot Cops.*

ERIC ANDREWS-KATZ (WriteOn530@gmail.com) lives in Seattle with his husband Alan. His work has appeared in *So Fey: Queer Fairy Fiction, The Best Date Ever, Charmed Lives: Gay Spirit in Storytelling* and *Gay City.* Eric's first novel *The Jesus Injection* and its sequel *Balls & Chain* are from Bold Strokes Books.

TOM BAKER is a graduate of the College of William and Mary who enjoyed an award-winning career in advertising. He is the author of the novel *The Sound of One Horse Dancing* and the story collection, *Full Frontal: to Make a Long Story Short*. His new novel is *Paper White Narcissus*.

SIMON BLEAKEN lives in Wiltshire, England. He frequently writes in the sci-fi, fantasy and horror genres, but enjoys letting his romantic side out for a whirl too. His fiction has appeared in several magazines, and in the anthologies: *Eldritch Horrors: Dark Tales* and *Space Horrors: Full-Throttle Spaces Tales #4*.

MICHAEL BRACKEN is the author of several books and more than one thousand short stories published in *Best Gay Romance 2010* and *2013*, *Best Gay Erotica 2013*, *Hot Blood: Strange Bedfellows*, *The Mammoth Book of Best New Erotica 4* and many other anthologies and periodicals. He lives and writes in Texas.

DALE CHASE has written male erotica for seventeen years. Her second novel, *Takedown: Taming John Wesley Hardin*, was published in 2013; her first, *Wyatt: Doc Holliday's Account of an Intimate Friendship*, came out in 2012. Dale has published several story collections and novellas while she continues to write for various anthologies.

CRAIG COTTER (craigcotter.com) is the author of three poetry collections including *Chopstix Numbers* and *After Lunch with Frank O'Hara*. His poetry has appeared in *Global Tapestry Review*, *poems-for-all*, *Poetry New Zealand*, *Assaracus*, *Court Green*, *Eleven Eleven*, *Euphony*, *The Antigonish Review* and *Caliban*; his prose has appeared in *Foolish Hearts*.

MICHAEL THOMAS FORD (michaelthomasford.com) is the author of numerous books, including the novels *Full Circle*,

Changing Tides, What We Remember, The Road Home and *Suicide Notes.* Winner of five Lambda Literary Awards and a finalist for the Bram Stoker Award, he is the recipient of the 2014 James Duggins Outstanding Mid-Career Novelist Prize.

DANIEL M. JAFFE is author of the novels *The Genealogy of Understanding* and *The Limits of Pleasure.* He also wrote *Jewish Gentle and Other Stories of Gay-Jewish Living,* compiled and edited *With Signs and Wonders: An International Anthology of Jewish Fabulist Fiction,* and translated the Russian-Israeli novel, *Here Comes The Messiah!* by Dina Rubina.

KEVIN KILLIAN lives in San Francisco where he has written fourteen books, including novels, poetry, nonfiction, plays and collections of short stories. Recent publications: a new novel, *Spreadeagle*; a collection of his color photographs, *Tagged: Variations on a Theme*; and a fourth book of stories, essays and memoirs, *Who Killed Teddy Bear?*

RAYMOND LUCZAK (raymondluczak.com) is the author and editor of fifteen books, including *How to Kill Poetry, Mute* and *Assembly Required: Notes from a Deaf Gay Life.* His novel *Men with Their Hands* won first place in the Project: QueerLit 2006 Contest. A playwright and filmmaker, he lives in Minneapolis, Minnesota.

GUILLERMO LUNA (misterdangerous.wordpress.com) had his first novel, *The Odd Fellows*, published in 2013. He received a BA in journalism from the University of Iowa and a master's degree in cinema from the University of Southern California. He also received a second master's degree from San Jose State University in library science.

ERIN MCRAE and **RACHELINE MALTESE**'s (Avian30.com) gay romance series *Love in Los Angeles,* set in the film and television industry, is published by Torquere Press. Racheline is a NYC-based performer and storyteller focused on themes of sex, gender, desire and mourning. Erin McRae is a writer and blogger based in Washington, D.C.

JAY MANDAL comes from southern England. He has written three novels: *The Dandelion Clock*, *Precipice* and *All About Sex*, and three collections: *A Different Kind of Love*, *The Loss of Innocence* and *Slubberdegullion*. His work has appeared in *Best Gay Romance 2009, 2010* and *2011*.

THOM NICKELS is the author of ten books, including: *Two Novellas: Walking Water & After All This, The Boy on the Bicycle, Manayunk, Gay and Lesbian Philadelphia, Out in History* and *Philadelphia Architecture.* He has written for The Huffington Post, *The New Oxford Review, Broad Street Review, The Philadelphia Inquirer* and others.

Editor of the Lambda Literary Award finalist *Tented: Gay Erotic Tales from Under the Big Top*, as well as four other erotica anthologies for Bold Strokes Books, **JERRY L. WHEELER**'s first collection of short fiction, *Strawberries and Other Erotic Fruits* was a Lambda Literary Award finalist in 2013.

ABOUT THE EDITOR

FELICE PICANO (felicepicano.net) is the author of thirty-five books of poetry, fiction, memoirs and nonfiction. His work is translated into sixteen languages; several titles were national and international bestsellers. Four of Picano's plays have been produced. He's considered a founder of modern gay literature along with other members of the Violet Quill. He's won or been nominated for numerous awards, including being a finalist for five Lambda Literary Awards in four categories. He received the City of West Hollywood's Rainbow Key award in 2013. Picano's recent work includes *20th Century Un-limited: Two Novellas (2013)*, *True Stories Too: People and Places From My Past (2014)* and *Nights at Rizzoli: a Memoir (2014)*.